对于从政有什么困难呢？”

【注 释】

1 季康子：季桓子之子，公元前492年继其父任鲁国正卿。孔子的弟子冉求，曾帮助季康子推行革新。

2 何有：有何困难。

【英译文】

Ji Kangzi asked whether Zhong You was the right person to put into office. The Master said, Zhong You is efficient. It goes without saying that he has the ability to hold office. Ji Kangzi said, How about Zi Gong? Would he be the right person to put into office? The Master said, He can turn his merits to account. It goes without saying, that he is capable of holding office. Ji Kangzi said, How about Ran Qiu? Would he be the right person to put into office? The Master said, He is versatile. It goes without saying that he is capable of holding office.

6.9

季氏使闵子骞[1]为费宰。闵子骞曰：“善为我辞焉！如有复我者，则吾必在汶上矣[2]。”

【中译文】

季氏派人去请闵子骞担任费邑的长官。闵子骞对来人说：“请替我婉言谢绝吧！如果再来请我，那我必定逃到汶水那边去了。”

【注 释】

1 闵子骞(qiān)：姓闵，名损，字子骞。鲁国人。公元前536年生，公元前487年卒(一说，公元前515－？)。孔子早年的弟子。相传是有名的孝子，受到孔子的赞赏。其德行与颜渊并称于世。费（bì)：是季氏的封邑，在今山东省费县西北(故城在平邑县东南七十里)。因为季氏不归顺鲁国，他的封邑的总管(邑宰，相当于一个县长)经常同他作对，所以，他想请闵子骞去做费宰。

2 在汶上：“汶(wèn)”，今山东省的大汶河。当时汶水在齐国的南面，鲁国的北面，流经齐鲁之间。在汶上，就是在汶水之上(汶水以北)，暗指要由鲁国去齐国，不愿为季氏做事。

【英译文】

The Ji family wanted to make Min Ziqian governor of Fei county Min Ziqian said, Invent a polite excuse for me. If that is not accepted and they try to get at me again, I shall certainly install myself on the far side of the Wen.

6.10

伯牛有疾[1]，子问之，自牖执其手[2]，曰：“亡之，命矣夫[3]！斯人也而有斯疾也，斯人也而有斯疾也！”

【中译文】

伯牛有病，孔子去探望，从窗户外面握住他的手，

说：“要是失去你，那真是命运呀！这样好的人竟得了这样的病啊！这样好的人竟得了这样的病啊！”

【注释】

1 伯牛：孔子的弟子。姓冉，名耕，字伯牛。鲁国人。孔子任鲁国司寇时，冉伯牛曾任中都宰，有德行。传说他患的是“癞病”(即麻疯病)，当时为不治之症。

2 牖(yǒu)：窗户。

3 夫(fú)：语气助词。表示感叹，相当于“吧”，“啊”。

【英译文】

When Bo Niu was ill, the Master went to see him, and grasping his hand through the window said, It is all over with him! Heaven has so ordained it -But that such a man should have such an illness! That such a man should have such anillness!

6.11

子曰：“贤哉，回也！一箪食[1]，一瓢饮，在陋巷，人不堪其忧，回也不改其乐。贤哉，回也！”

【中译文】

孔子说：“贤良呀，颜回！一竹筒饭，一瓢水，住

在狭小的巷子里，一般人都忍受不了那种困苦忧愁，颜回却不改变他的快乐。贤良呀，颜回！”

【注释】

1 箪(dān)：古时盛饭食用的一种圆形竹器。食(sì)：饭。

【英译文】

The Master (Confucius) said, Incomparable indeed was Yan Hui! A handful of rice to eat, a gourdful of water to drink, living in a mean street. Others would have found it unendurably depressing, but to Hui's cheerfulness it made no difference at all. Incomparable indeed was Yan Hui!

6.12

冉求曰：“非不说子之道[1]，力不足也。”子曰：“力不足者，中道而废，今女画[2]。”

【中译文】

冉求对孔子说：“不是我不喜欢您的思想学说，而是我的实践的能力有限。”孔子说：“能力有限的话，是半途而废，但现在你却先自我限制，裹足不前。”

【注释】

1 说：同：“悦”。喜欢，爱慕。

2 女：同“汝”。你。画：画线为界。

【英译文】

Ran Qiu said, It is not that your Way does not comment itself to me, but that it demands powers I do not possess. The Master said, He whose strength gives out collapses during the course of the journey(the Way); but you deliberately draw the line.

6.13

子谓子夏曰："女为君子儒[1]，无为小人儒。"

【中译文】

孔子对子夏说："你要做君子式的读书人，不要做小人式的读书人。"

【注释】

1 女：你。

【英译文】

The Master (Confucius) said to Zi Xia, You must be a scholar of gentlemen, not of petty men.

6.14

子游为武城宰[1]。子曰："女得人焉耳乎[2]？"曰："有澹台灭明者[3]，行不由径[4]，非公事，未

尝至于偃之室也[5]。"

【中译文】

子游做武城地方的官长。孔子问："在你管的地区你发现什么人才了吗？"子游答："有个名叫澹台灭明的人，做事从来不抄小道，不是为公事，从不到我的私宅来。"

【注释】

1 武城：鲁国的城邑。即今山东省嘉祥县。一说，武城在山东省费县西南。

2 焉耳：犹言"于此"。"耳"，同"尔"。

3 澹(tán)台灭明：姓澹台，名灭明，字子羽。武城人。为人公正。后来成为孔子的弟子。传说澹台灭明状貌甚丑，孔子曾以为他才薄。而后，澹台灭明受业修行，名闻于世。孔子叹说："吾以貌取人，失之子羽。"

4 径：小路，捷径。引申为正路之外的邪路。行：做事。

5 偃：即子游。姓言名偃，字子游。这里是子游自称。

【英译文】

When Zi You was the governor of Wu County, the Master said, Have you managed to get hold of the right sort of people there? Zi You said, There is someone called Dantai Mieming who 'walks on no bypaths'. He has not once come to my house except on public business.

6.15

子曰："孟之反不伐[1]。奔而殿[2]，将入门，策其马[3]，曰：'非敢后也，马不进也。'"

【中译文】

孔子说："孟之反不自我夸耀。败退时，他护后，将要进城门时，他拍拍马说：'不是我敢于在后，是马跑不快。'"

【注释】

1 孟之反：姓孟，名侧，字之反(《左传》作"孟之侧"，《庄子》作"孟子反")。鲁国的大夫。伐：夸耀功劳。

2 奔：败走。殿：殿后，即行军走在最后。鲁哀公十一年(公元前484年)，齐国进攻鲁国，鲁迎战，季氏宰冉求所率领的右翼军队战败。撤退时，众军争先奔走，而孟之反却在最后作掩护。故孔子称赞孟之反：人有功不难，不夸功为难。

3 策：鞭打。

【英译文】

The Master (Confucius) said, Meng Zhifan is no boaster. When his people were routed he was the last to flee; but when they neared the city-gate, he whipped up his horsed and said, It was not courage that kept me behind. My horses were slow.

6.16

子曰："不有祝鮀之佞[1]，而有宋朝之美[2]，难乎免于今世矣。"

【中译文】

孔子说："如果没有祝鮀的能言善辩，没有宋朝那样的美貌，在当今之世是难以免遭灾祸的。"

【注释】

1 祝鮀(tuó)：姓祝，名鮀，字子鱼。卫国的大夫。因他擅长外交辞令，能言善辩，而又会阿谀逢迎，受到卫灵公的重用。

2 而：同"与"。和，二者兼有。宋朝：不是宋代而是宋国的公子朝，貌美闻名于世。《左传·昭公二十年》及《定公十四年》记述公子朝与襄夫人宣姜私通，并参与发动祸乱，出奔到卫国。又以貌美，与卫灵公夫人南子私通，而受到宠幸。

【英译文】

The Master (Confucius) said, Without the eloquence of the priest T'o and the beauty of Prince Chao of Song State it is hard nowadays to get through.

6.17

子曰："谁能出不由户[1]？何莫由斯道也[2]？"

【中译文】

孔子说："谁能外出而不经过屋门呢？为什么不正常从屋门出入呢？"

【注释】

1 户：门。

2 何莫：为什么没有。斯道：这条路。这里指仁义之道，其实是每个人的立身之本，但多为人所忽略乃至摒弃。

【英译文】

The Master (Confucius) said, Who expects to be able to go out of a house except by the door? Then why won't people follow my way?

6.18

子曰："质胜文则野[1]，文胜质则史[2]。文质彬彬[3]，然后君子。"

【中译文】

孔子说："内在的质地胜过外在的文采，就未免粗野；外在的文采胜过内在的质地，就未免浮夸虚伪。只有把文采与质朴配合恰当，然后才能成为君子。"

【注释】

1 质：质地，质朴、朴实的内容，内在的思想感情。孔子认为，仁义是质。文：文采，华丽的装饰，外在的礼仪。孔子认为，礼乐是文。

2 史：本义是宗庙里掌礼仪的祝官，官府里掌文书的史官。这里指像"史"那样，言词华丽，虚浮铺陈，心里并无诚意。含有浮夸虚伪的贬义。

3 彬彬：文质兼备相称；文与质互相融和，配合恰当。

【英译文】

The Master (Confucius) said, When natural substance prevails over ornamentation, you get the boorishness of the rustic. When ornamentation prevails over natural substance, you get the pedantry of the scribe. Only when ornament and substance are duly blended do you get the true gentleman.

6.19

子曰："人之生也直[1]，罔之生也幸而免[2]。"

【中译文】

孔子说："一个人的存在，必须过正直的生活；不正直的人能存在，不过是由于侥幸而躲过了惩罚。"

【注释】

1 直：正直，无私曲。

2 罔(wǎng)：诬罔，虚妄。指不正直的人。

【英译文】

The Master (Confucius) said, Man's very life is honesty, in that without it he will be lucky indeed if he escapes with his life.

6.20

子曰："知之者不如好[1]之者[2]，好之者不如乐之者。"

【中译文】

孔子说："知道它的人，不如喜欢它的人；喜欢它的人，不如实践并以之为快乐的人。"

【注释】

1 好(hào)：喜欢。

2 之：此处指道。

【英译文】

The Master (Confucius) said, To prefer it is better than only to know it. To delight in it is better than merely to prefer it.

6.21

子曰："中人以上，可以语上也[1]；中人以下，不可以语上也。"

【中译文】

孔子说："对有中等资质的人，可以讲高深的知识学问；对中等资质以下的人，不可以讲那些高深的知识学问。"

【注释】

1 语：告，讲，说。此处主张因材施教。

【英译文】

The Master (Confucius) said, To men who are above average, one may talk of things higher yet. But to men who are below average, one may not.

6.22

樊迟问知[1]，子曰："务民之义[2]，敬鬼神而远之，可谓知矣。"问仁，曰："仁者先难而后获，可谓仁矣。"

【中译文】

樊迟问如何才算智慧，孔子说："做老百姓需要做的事情，尊敬鬼神，但同时保持距离与之，就可以说是智慧了。"樊迟又问怎样才是"仁"，孔子说："有仁德的人，艰苦在先，酬报在后，便可以说是'仁'啊。"

【注释】

1 知：同"智"。聪明，智慧。

2 务：从事于，致力于，一心一意去专力倡导。

【英译文】

Fan Chi asked about wisdom. The Master said, The man who devotes himself to securing for his subjects what it is right they should have, who by respect for the Spirits keeps them at a distance, may be termed wise. He asked about Goodness. The Master said, Goodness cannot be obtained till what is difficult has been duly done. The man who has done this may be called Good.

6.23

子曰："知者乐水[1]，仁者乐山[2]。知者动，仁者静。知者乐，仁者寿。"

【中译文】

孔子说："有智慧的人喜欢水，有仁德的人喜欢山。有智慧的人活跃，有仁德的人沉静。有智慧的人常乐，有仁德的人长寿。"

【注释】

1 知者乐水：水流动而不板滞，随岸赋形，随机应变，与智者相似，故曰。乐：喜欢。

2 仁者乐山：山形巍然，屹立而不动摇，有所持守不易改变，与仁者相似，故曰。

【英译文】

The Master (Confucius) said, The wise man delights in water, the Good man delights in mountains. For the wise move; but the Good stay still. The

wise are happy; but the Good are long-lived.

6.24

子曰："齐一变，至于鲁；鲁一变，至于道[1]。"

【中译文】

孔子说："把齐国政治改善一下，便达到像鲁国这样；把鲁国政治改善一下，就能达到先王之道了。"

【注释】

1 "齐一变"句："变，"进行政治改革，推行教化。鲁保留的周代礼制和风习比齐更深。孔子曾说："周礼尽在鲁矣。"

【英译文】

The Master (Confucius) said, A single change could bring chi state to the level of Lu state; and a single change would bring Lu to the way.

6.25

子曰："觚不觚，觚哉？觚哉[1]？"

【中译文】

孔子说："说是酒杯又不像酒杯，这是酒杯吗？这是酒杯吗？"

【注释】

1 “觚不觚”句：“觚(gū)”，古代木制酒具，容量为古制二升(一说三升)，量不大，以戒人贪酒。原先觚是上圆下方，腹部足部都有四条棱角。后来，可能是为了制造和使用上的方便，改成了圆筒形，也没有那四条棱角了。孔子言“觚不觚”，实是对事物有所改变、有名无实、名实不符的感叹。

【英译文】

The Master (Confucius) said, A horn-gourd that is neither horn nor gourd! A pretty horn-gourd indeed, a pretty horn-gourd indeed.

6.26

宰我问曰：“仁者，虽告之曰：‘井有仁焉[1]。’其从之也？”子曰：“何为其然也？君子可逝也[2]不可陷也；可欺也，不可罔也[3]。”

【中译文】

宰我问道：“对于有仁德的人，如果告诉他：‘有一位仁人掉到井里啦！’他会跟着跳下去吗？”孔子说：“为什么要他那样做呢？可以使他去井边看一看，不可能使他下井去；君子可能被欺骗，却不会被愚弄。”

【注释】

1 井有仁：井里掉进一个有仁德的人。一说，“仁”同“人”。

2 逝：往，去。

3 罔：诬罔，被无理陷害，愚弄。

【英译文】

Zai Wo asked, I take it a Good Man, even if he were told that another Good Man were at the bottom of a well, would go to join him? The Master said, Why should you think so? 'A gentleman can be broken, but cannot be dented; may be deceived, but cannot be led astray.'

6.27

子曰：“君子博学于文，约之以礼，亦可以弗畔矣夫[1]！”

【中译文】

孔子说：“君子以知识丰富自己，用礼来约束自己，就可以不违背事理了！”

【注释】

1 畔：同“叛”。背离，背叛。夫(fú)：语气助词。吧。

【英译文】

The Master (Confucius) said, A gentleman who is widely versed in letters and at the same time knows how to submit his learning to the restraints of ritual is not likely, to go far wrong.

6.28

子见南子[1]，子路不说[2]。夫子矢之曰[3]：“予所否者[4]，天厌之！天厌之！”

【中译文】

孔子会见了南子，子路不高兴。孔子发誓说：“假如我做了什么错事，上天会弃绝我！上天会弃绝我！”

【注释】

1 南子：宋国的美女，卫灵公的夫人，行为淫乱，名声不好。当时，卫灵公年老昏庸，南子实际上操纵、左右着卫国的政权。她派人召见孔子，孔子起初辞谢不见，但因依礼当见，不得已才去见了南子。

2 说：同“悦”。

3 矢：通：“誓”。

4 予所否者：“予”，我。“所……者”，相当于“假如…… 的话”，古代用于誓言中。“否”，不是，不对。指做了什么错误的事情。

【英译文】

When the Master went to see Nan Zi, Zi Lu was not pleased. Where upon the Master made a solemn declaration concerning his visit, saying, If I have done amiss, may Heaven avert it , may Heaven avert it!

6.29

子曰：“中庸之为德也[1]，甚至矣乎！民鲜久矣 。”

【中译文】

孔子说：“中庸作为一种道德，是最高尚了！人民缺少这种道德已经很久了。”

【注释】

1 中庸：“中”，是折中，调和，无过无不及，不偏不倚；“庸”，是平常，普通，循常规常理(顺其 自然)而不变。所以程子说：“不偏之谓中，不易之谓庸。”

【英译文】

The Master (Confucius) said, How transcendent is the moral power of the Middle Use! That it is but rarely found among the common people is a fact long admitted.

6.30

子贡曰："如有博施于民而能济众，何如？可谓仁乎？"子曰："何事于仁，必也圣乎！尧、舜其犹病诸[1]。夫仁者，己欲立而立人，己欲达而达人。能近取譬[2]，可谓仁之方也已。

【中译文】

子贡说："如果有人给广大人民带来利益，又能周济众人，怎么样呢？可以说是仁人吗？"孔子说："何止是仁人，那必定是圣人了！尧、舜都很难做到。作为仁人，自己想要立身，就要帮助别人立身；自己想要通达，也要帮助别人通达。从近处做起，可以说是实行仁的方法啊。"

【注释】

1 尧、舜：传说是上古两位贤明的君主，也是孔子心目中圣德典范。病：忧虑，犯难，心有所不足。

2 能近取譬："近"，指切近的生活，自身。"譬"，比喻，比方。能够就自身打比方，推己及人。

【英译文】

Zi Gong asked, "What would you say of a man if he not only conferred wide benefits upon the common people, but also accomplished the salvation of the whole state? Could such a man be called the best way to implement benevolence?" The Master said, "It would no longer be a matter of benevolence. He would without doubt be a sage! Even Yao and Shun found it hard to do so. I would like to describe benevolence like this: You yourself desire standing, then help others to get standing. You yourself want success, then help others to succeed. To be able to draw analogies from oneself may be called benevolence."

述而篇第七（共三十八章）

About Confucius Being Modest

7.1

子曰：“述而不作[1]，信而好古，窃比于我老彭[2]。”

【中译文】

孔子说：“只阐述古代文化典籍而不创作，相信而且喜爱古代文化，我私自把自己比作老彭。”

【注释】

1 述：传述，阐述。作：创造，创作。

2 窃：私下，私自。第一人称的谦称。我老彭：“老彭”指彭祖，传说姓篯（jiān），名铿，是颛顼（五帝之一）之孙陆终氏的后裔，封于彭城（今徐州），仕虞、夏、商三代，至殷王时已七百六十七岁（一说长寿达八百岁）。彭祖是有名的贤大夫，自少爱恬静养生，观览古书，好述古事（见《神仙传》、《列仙传》、《庄子》）。“老彭”前加“我”，是表示了孔子对“老彭”的尊敬与亲切，如同说“我的老彭”。一说，“老彭”指老子和彭祖两个人。

【英译文】

The Master (Confucius) said, I have 'transmitted what was taught to me

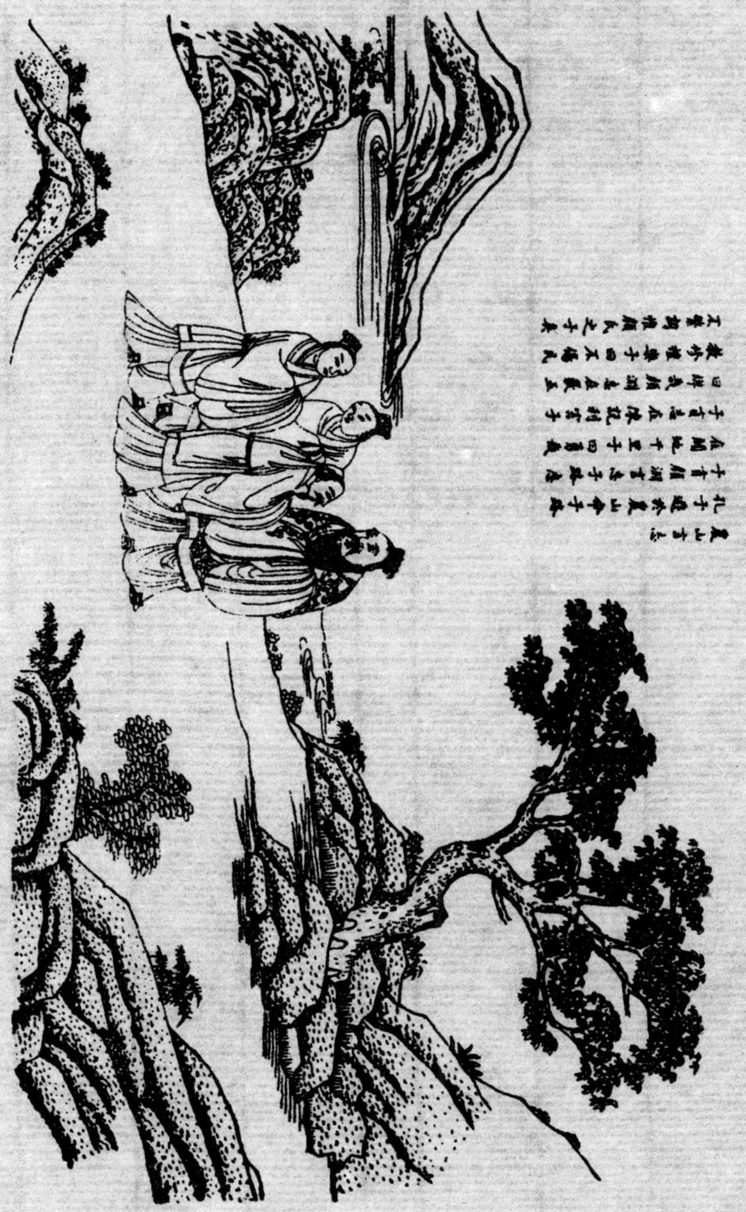

农山言志 Expressing Ambitions on Nong Mountain

without making up anything of my own'. I have been faithful to and loved the Ancients. In these respects, I make bold to think.

7.2

子曰："默而识之[1]，学而不厌[2]，诲人不倦[3]，何有于我哉[4]？"

【中译文】

孔子说："默默地体会所学的知识，勤奋学习永不满足，耐心地教导别人而不倦怠，这些我做到了吗？"

【注释】

1 识（zhì）：牢记，记住。潜心思考，加以辨别，存之于心。

2 厌：通"餍"。本义是饱食。引申为满足，厌烦。

3 诲（huì）：教诲，教导，诱导。

4 "何有"句：即"于我何有哉"。这是孔子严格要求自己的谦虚之词，意思说：以上那几方面，我做 到了哪些（一说，还有什么困难或遗憾）呢？

【英译文】

not even our old Peng can have excelled me. The Master said, I have listened in silence and noted what was said, I have never grown tired of learning nor wearied of teaching others what I have learnt. These at least are merits which I can confidently claim.

7.3

子曰："德之不修，学之不讲，闻义不能徙[1]，不善不能改[2]，是吾忧也。"

【中译文】

孔子说："品德不去修养，学问不去讲授，知道应做的却不能去做，对缺点错误不能改正，这些都是我所忧虑的。"

【注释】

1 义：这里指正义的、合乎道义义理的事。徙（xǐ）：本义是迁移。这里指徙而从之，使自己的所做所为靠近义，做到实践义，走向义。

2 不善：不好。指缺点，错误。

【英译文】

The Master (Confucius) said, The thought that 'I have left my moral power untended, my learning unperfected, that I have heard of righteous men, but been unable to go to them; have heard of evil men, but been unable to reform them'-these are what I am concerned about.

7.4

子之燕居[1]，申申如也[2]，夭夭如也[3]。

【中译文】

孔子在家闲暇无事时，容貌舒展而安详。

【注释】

1 燕居："燕"，通"宴"。安逸，闲适。燕居，指独自闲暇无事的时候的安居、家居。

2 申申：容貌舒展安详的样子。如也：像是……的样子。

3 夭夭（yāo）：脸色和悦愉快，斯文自在，轻松舒畅的样子。

【英译文】

When the Master was at home, his manner was very free-and-easy, and his expression alert and cheerful.

7.5

子曰："甚矣吾衰也，久矣吾不复梦见周公[1]。"

【中译文】

孔子说："我真衰老了啊，很久我没再梦见周公了。"

【注释】

1 周公：姓姬，名旦。是周文王（姬昌）的儿子，周武王（姬发）的弟弟，周成王（姬诵）的叔叔，也是鲁国国君的始祖。传说周公是西周政治礼乐典章制度的制定者，他辅佐周成王，安天下，有德政，是孔子所崇尚的先圣先贤之一。孔子从年轻时就欲行周公之道，但壮志至老未酬。这里表现了孔子对心有余而力不足，政治抱负已不可能实现的慨叹。

【英译文】

The Master (Confucius) said, How utterly have things gone to the bad with me! It is a long time indeed since I dreamed that I saw the Duke Zhou.

7.6

子曰："志于道，据于德，依于仁，游于艺[1]。"

【中译文】

孔子说："以道作为志向，以德作为根据，以仁作为凭藉，游习于六艺之中。"

【注释】

1 游：这里有玩习，熟悉的意思。艺：六艺。指礼（礼节），乐（音乐），射（射箭），御（驾车），书（写　字），数（算术）。孔子用这六个方面的知识技艺来培养教授学生。

【英译文】

The Master (Confucius) said, Set your heart upon the Way, support yourself by virtue, lean upon Goodness, seek distraction in the arts.

7.7

子曰：“自行束脩以上[1]，吾未尝无诲焉[2]。”

【中译文】

孔子说：“只要愿意主动带点见面礼表示尊重而来问学的人，我从来没有不教诲的。”

【注释】

1 行：实行，做到。束脩：“脩（xīu）”，干肉。束脩，是捆在一起的一束干肉。每束十条。古代人们常用来作为见面的薄礼。

2 未尝：未曾，从来没有。

【英译文】

The Master (Confucius) said, From the very poorest upwards-beginning even with the man who could bring no better present than a bundle of dried meat-none has ever come to me without receiving instruction.

7.8

子曰：“不愤不启[1]，不悱不发[2]，举一隅不以三隅反[3]，则不复也。”

【中译文】

孔子说：“教导学生不到他苦思冥想而仍领会不了的时候，不去启发他；不到他想说而又说不出来的时

候，不去开导他。告诉他屋子的一个角，他不能由此推知另外三个角，就不再去教他了。”

【注释】

1 愤：思考问题有疑难之处，苦思冥想，而仍然没想通，仍然领会不了的样子。

2 悱（fěi）：想说而不能明确地表达，说不出来的样子。

3 隅（yú）：角落，角。这里比喻从已知的一点，去进行推论，由此及彼，触类旁通。这句就是成语“举一反三”和“启发”一词的由来。

【英译文】

The Master (Confucius)said, Only one who bursts with eagerness do I instruct; only one who bubbles with excitement, do I enlighten. If I hold up one corner and a man cannot come back to me with the other three, I do not continue the lesson.

7.9

子食于有丧者之侧[1]，未尝饱也。

【中译文】

孔子在家有丧事的人旁边吃饭，从未吃饱过。

【注释】

1 有丧者：有丧事的人。指刚刚死去亲属的人家。孔子在有丧事的人面前，因同情失去亲人的人，食欲不振，吃饭无味，故云“未尝饱也”。

7.7

子曰："自行束脩以上¹，吾未尝无诲焉²。"

【中译文】

孔子说："只要愿意主动带点见面礼表示尊重而来问学的人，我从来没有不教诲的。"

【注释】

1 行：实行，做到。束脩："脩（xiū）"，干肉。束脩，是捆在一起的一束干肉。每束十条。古代人们常用来作为见面的薄礼。

2 未尝：未曾，从来没有。

【英译文】

The Master (Confucius) said. From the very poorest upwards-beginning even with the man who could bring no better present than a bundle of dried meat-none has ever come to me without receiving instruction.

7.8

子曰："不愤不启¹，不悱不发²，举一隅不以三隅反³，则不复也。"

【中译文】

孔子说："教导学生不到他苦思冥想而仍领会不了的时候，不去启发他；不到他想说而又说不出来的时候，不去开导他。告诉他屋子的一个角，他不能由此推知另外三个角，就不再去教他了。"

【注释】

1 愤：思考问题有疑难之处，苦思冥想，而仍然没想通，仍然领会不了的样子。

2 悱（fěi）：想说而不能明确地表达，说不出来的样子。

3 隅（yú）：角落，角。这里比喻从已知的一点，去进行推论，由此及彼，触类旁通。这句就是成语"举一反三"和"启发"一词的由来。

【英译文】

The Master (Confucius) said. Only one who bursts with eagerness do I instruct; only one who bubbles with exetement, do I enlighten. If I hold up one corner and a man cannot come back to me with the other three, I do not continue the lesson.

7.9

子食于有丧者之侧¹，未尝饱也。

【中译文】

孔子在死了亲属的人旁边吃饭，从来没有吃饱过。

【注释】

1 有丧者：有丧事的人。指刚刚死去亲属的人家。孔子在有丧事的人面前，因同情失去亲人的人，食欲不振，吃饭无味，故云"未尝饱也"。

甘于寂寞。只有我和你能够做到这样吧！”子路说：“您如果统帅部队去作战，那么，您要和谁在一起呢？”孔子说：“赤手空拳和老虎搏斗，徒步趟水过大河，死了都不知后悔的人，我不和他在一起。与我共事的人必须是遇事小心谨慎，严肃认真，善于筹划谋略而能争取成功的人。”

【注释】

1 舍：不用，舍弃。

2 行：视，居……之位。这里犹言指挥，统帅。三军：当时一个大国的所有军队。每军一万二千五百人，三军相当于三万七千五百人。

3 与：在一起，共事。

4 暴虎冯河：“暴”，徒手搏击。句中指赤手空拳与老虎搏斗。“冯(píng)”，涉水。句中指无船而徒步趟水过大河。暴虎冯河，是用来比喻那种有勇无谋，冒险行事，而往往导致失败的人。

【英译文】

The Master (Confucius) said to Yan Hui, When wanted, then go; When set aside; then hide. Only you and I could certainly fulfil. Zi Lu said, Supposing you had command of the Three Hosts, whom would you take to help you? The Master said, The man who was ready to 'beard a tiger or rush a river' without caring whether he lived or died -that sort of man I should not take. I should certainly take someone who approached difficulties with due caution and who preferred to succeed by strategy.

【英译文】

If at a meal the Master found himself seated next to someone who was in mourning, he never eat his fill.

7.10

子于是日哭[1]，则不歌。

【中译文】

孔子在那一天吊丧哭泣过，就不再唱歌了。

【注释】

1 哭：指给别人吊丧时哭泣。一日之内，由于心里悲痛，余哀未忘，就不会再唱歌了。

【英译文】

When he had wailed at a funeral, during the rest of the day he did not sing.

7.11

子谓颜渊曰：“用之则行，舍之则藏[1]，惟我与尔有是夫！”子路曰：“子行三军[2]，则谁与[3]？”子曰：“暴虎冯河[4]，死而无悔者，吾不与也。必也临事而惧，好谋而成者也。”

【中译文】

孔子对颜渊说：“得到重用就好好干，不得重用就

【英译文】

If at a meal the Master found himself seated next to someone who was in mourning, he never ate his fill.

7.10

子于是日哭[1]，则不歌。

【中译文】

孔子在那一天吊丧哭泣过，就不再唱歌了。

【注释】

1 哭：指给别人吊丧时哭泣。一日之内，由于心里悲痛，余哀未忘，就不会再唱歌了。

【英译文】

When he had wailed at a funeral, during the rest of the day he did not sing.

7.11

子谓颜渊曰："用之则行，舍之则藏[1]，惟我与尔有是夫！"子路曰："子行三军[2]，则谁与[3]？"子曰："暴虎冯河[4]，死而无悔者，吾不与也。必也临事而惧，好谋而成者也。"

【中译文】

孔子对颜渊说："得到重用就好好干，不得重用就甘于寂寞。只有我和你能够做到这样吧！"子路说："您如果统帅部队去作战，那么，您要和谁在一起呢？"孔子说："赤手空拳和老虎搏斗，徒步趟水过大河，死了都不知后悔的人，我不和他在一起。与我共事的人必须是遇事小心谨慎，严肃认真，善于筹划谋略而能争取成功的人。"

【注释】

1 舍：不用，舍弃。

2 行：做，居……之位。这里姑言指挥，统帅。三军：当时一个大国的所有军队。每军一万二千五百人，三军相当于三万七千五百人。

3 与：在一起，共事。

4 暴虎冯河："暴"，徒手搏击。句中指赤手空拳与老虎搏斗。"冯(píng)"，涉水。句中指无船而徒步趟水过大河。暴虎冯河，是用来比喻那种有勇无谋，冒险行事，而往往导致失败的人。

【英译文】

The Master (Confucius) said to Yan Hui, When wanted, then go; When set aside; then hide. Only you and I could certainly fulfil. Zi Lu said, Supposing you had command of the Three Hosts, whom would you take to help you? The Master said, The man who was ready to 'beard a tiger or rush a river' without caring whether he lived or died - that sort of man I should not take. I should certainly take someone who approached difficulties with due caution and who preferred to succeed by strategy.

7.12

子曰："富而可求也，虽执鞭之士[1]，吾亦为之。如不可求，从吾所好[2]。"

【中译文】

孔子说："财富如果是可以求得的，就是去当马车夫，我也愿意去做。如果不可以求得，我还是做我喜欢做的事。"

【注释】

1 执鞭之士：指手里拿着皮鞭的下等差役。当时主要指两种人，一种是市场的守门人，执鞭以维持秩序；一种是为贵族外出时夹道执鞭开路、让行人让道的差役。

2 从：顺从，听从。

【英译文】

The Master (Confucius) said, If any means of escaping poverty presented itself that did not involve doing wrong, I would adopt it, even though my employment were only that of the gentleman who holds the whip. But so long as it is a question of illegitimate means, I shall continue to pursue what I love.

7.13

子之所慎：齐[1]，战[2]，疾[3]。

【中译文】

孔子小心谨慎对待的事情是：斋戒，战争，疾病。

【注释】

1 齐：同"斋"。指古代在祭祀之前虔诚的斋戒。要求不喝酒，不吃荤，不与妻妾同房，沐浴净身，等等，以达到身心的全面整洁。

2 战：战争。因关系国家民族的安危存亡和人民群众的死与伤。

3 疾：疾病。因关系个人的健康与生死。

【英译文】

The Master (Confucius) gave the greatest attention as to three things: fasting, war and sickness.

7.14

子在齐，闻《韶》[1]，三月不知肉味[2]，曰："不图为乐之至于斯也。"

【中译文】

孔子在齐国，听到了演奏《韶》乐后，三个月吃肉都不知滋味，说："真料想不到音乐所带来的快乐能到如此境地。"

【注释】

1 韶：传说是虞舜时创作的乐曲，水平很高，音乐境

姓蒯(kuǎi)，名辄(zhé)。公元前492年至公元前481年在位。他的父亲蒯聩，本是灵公所立的世子，但因其谋杀卫灵公的夫人南子未成，被灵公驱逐，逃到了晋国。卫灵公死后，蒯辄被立为国君。这时，晋国的赵简子率军又把蒯聩送回卫国，形成父亲同儿子争夺王位的局面。后来蒯聩以武力进攻其子蒯辄，蒯辄出奔。蒯聩得王位，为卫庄公。公元前478年，晋攻卫，蒯聩奔戎州，被戎州人所杀。蒯辄奔宋之后，卒于越。蒯聩、蒯辄父子争位的事，与古代伯夷、叔齐两兄弟互相让位的事，形成了鲜明的对比。本章这段对话，表明孔子赞扬伯夷、叔齐的"礼让为国"，而对蒯聩、蒯辄非常不满。

2 诺：应答声。

【英译文】

Ran You said, Is our Master on the side of the prince of Wei? Zi Gong said, yes, I'll ask him about that. He went in and said, What kind of people were Bo Yi and Shu Qi? The Master said, "They were ancient sages." Zi Gong said, "Did they regret their actions?" The Master said, "They sought benevolence and obtained it. Why should they have had regrets?" Zi Gong came out and said, "Our Master is not on his side."

7.16

子曰："饭疏食[1]，饮水，曲肱而枕之[2]，乐亦在其中矣。不义而富且贵，于我如浮云。"

界很优美。参见前《八佾篇第三》第二十五章注。

2 三月：比喻很长时间，不是实指三个月。

【英译文】

When he was in Qi state, the Master heard Shao music, and for three months did not know the taste of meat. He said I did not picture to myself that any music existed which could reach such perfection as this.

7.15

冉有曰："夫子为卫君乎[1]？"子贡曰："诺[2]，吾将问之。"入，曰："伯夷、叔齐何人也？"曰："古之贤人也。"曰："怨乎？"曰："求仁而得仁，又何怨？"出，曰："夫子不为也。"

【中译文】

冉有问子贡说："老师会赞成卫国的国君吗？"子贡说："嗯，我要去问问他。"于是，子贡进屋去问孔子："伯夷、叔齐是什么样的人呢？"孔子说："是古代的贤人。"子贡问："伯夷、叔齐会有什么怨悔吗？"孔子说："他们求仁德而得到了仁德，还有什么怨悔呢？"子贡走出屋来对冉有说："老师不赞成卫国国君。"

【注释】

1 为：赞成，帮助。卫君：指卫灵公的孙子卫出公，

【中译文】

孔子说："吃粗粮，喝冷水，弯起胳膊当枕头，乐趣就在其中了。用不义的手段得到富与贵，对我来说，就像天上的浮云。"

【注释】

1 饭：作动词用。吃。疏食：指粗粮，粗糙的饭食。

2 肱(gōng)：由肩到胳膊肘这一部位，一般也泛指胳膊。

【英译文】

The Master (Confucius)said, The man who seeks only coarse food to eat, water to drink and a bent arm for pillow, will without looking for it find happiness to boot, Any thought of accepting wealth and rank by means that I knows to be wrong is as remote from me as the floating clouds.

7.17

子曰："加我数年[1]，五十以学《易》[2]，可以无大过矣。"

【中译文】

孔子说："再给我数年时光，五十岁研习《易经》，就可以做到不犯大的错误了。"

【注释】

1 加：增添，增加。

2 五十：五十岁。古人以为五十岁是老年的开始。一说，"五十"是"卒"字之误，在这里用的意思，指学完《易经》。易：又名《周易》。

【英译文】

The Master (Confucius)said, Give me a few more years, so that I may have spent a whole fifty in studying 'the Book of changes'. and I believe that after all I should be fairly free from errors.

7.18

子所雅言[1]，《诗》、《书》、执礼，皆雅言也。

【中译文】

孔子常使用的正式语言，多出自《诗经》，《尚书》，包括履行礼仪时，都经常用到。

【注释】

1 雅言：朱熹注《伦语》：雅、常也，经常使用的语言。

【英译文】

The occasions upon which the Master used correct pronunciation were when reciting the Songs or the Books and when practising ritual acts. At all such times he used the correct pronunciation.

7.19

叶公问孔子于子路[1]，子路不对[2]。子曰：“女奚不曰[3]：其为人也，发愤忘食，乐以忘忧，不知老之将至云尔[4]。”

【中译文】

叶公向子路问到孔子，子路没回答。孔子说：“你为什么不说：他的为人啊，发愤读书时，竟忘记吃饭；快乐时，便忘记忧愁；乃至于常常忘了自己快老了，如此而已。”

【注释】

1 叶(shè)公：姓沈，名诸梁，字子高，楚国的大夫。他的封邑在叶城(今河南省叶县南三十里有古叶城)，为叶尹，故称叶公。

2 不对：不回答。“对”，是应答之意。

3 女：同“汝”。你。奚：何，为什么。

4 云尔：如此而已，罢了。

【英译文】

Duke She asked Zi Lu about Confucius Zi Lu did not reply. The Master said, Why did you not say 'This is the character of the man: so intent upon enlightening the eager that he forgets his hunger, and so happy in doing so, that he forgets the bitterness of his lot and does not realize that old age is at hand. That is what he is.'

7.20

子曰：“我非生而知之者，好古，敏以求之者也。”

【中译文】

孔子说：“我不是生下来就有知识，而是爱好古代文化，勤奋探索而获得知识的人。”

【英译文】

The Master said, I wasn't born with innate knowledge. I am simply one who loves the past and who is diligent in seeking it.

7.21

子不语怪、力、乱、神。

【中译文】

孔子不谈论怪异、暴力、悖乱、鬼神一类的事。

【英译文】

The Master (Confucius) never talked of prodigies, feats of strength, disorders or spirits.

7.22

子曰：“三人行，必有我师焉。择其善者而

从之，其不善者而改之。”

【中译文】

孔子说：“如果三个人在一起走，其中必定有可以作为我老师的人。选择他的优点加以学习；看到有什么不好的地方，就反省自己加以改正。”

【英译文】

The Master (Confucius) said, Even when walking in a party of no more than three I can always be certain of learning from those I am with. There will be good qualities that I can select for imitation and bad ones that will teach me what requires correction in myself.

7.23

子曰：“天生德于予，桓魋其如予何[1]！”

【中译文】

孔子说：“上天赋予我道德并代之宣化，桓魋能把我怎么样！”

【注释】

1 桓魋(tuí)：宋国的司马(主管军事行政的长官)。本名向魋，因是宋桓公的后裔，又称桓魋。公元前492年，孔子周游列国，从卫国去陈国时，经过宋国，桓魋听到消息，率兵来阻拦。当时，孔子正在大树下同弟子们演习周礼的仪式，桓魋砍掉大树，而且要杀孔子。孔子离开时，弟子们催促他快些走，他在途中说了这番话。

【英译文】

The Master (Confucius) said, Heaven begat the power that is in me. What have I to fear from such a one as Huan Tui?

7.24

子曰：“二三子以我为隐乎[1]？吾无隐乎尔。吾无行而不与二三子者，是丘也。”

【中译文】

孔子说：“诸位以为我对你们有什么隐瞒吗？我没有隐瞒啊。我没有什么行为不能公开的，这就是我孔丘啊。”

【注释】

1 二三子：这里是孔子客气地称呼弟子们。“二三”，表示约数。“子”，是尊称。

【英译文】

The Master (Confucius) said, My friends, I know you think that there is something I am keeping from you. There is nothing at all that I keep from you. I take no steps about which I do not consult you, my friends. Were it otherwise, I should not be Chiu.

7.25

子以四教：文[1]，行[2]，忠[3]，信[4]。

【中译文】

孔子从四个方面教育学生：文献，行为，忠诚，信用。

【注释】

1 文：文化知识，历史文献。
2 行：行为规范，道德修养，社会实践。
3 忠：忠诚老实。
4 信：讲信用，言行一致。

【英译文】

The Master (Confucius) took four subjects for his teaching: culture, conduct of affairs, loyalty to superiors, and the keeping of promises.

7.26

子曰："圣人，吾不得而见之矣，得见君子者，斯可矣[1]。"子曰："善人，吾不得而见之矣，得见有恒者，斯可矣。亡而为有[2]，虚而为盈[3]，约而为泰[4]，难乎有恒矣。"

【中译文】

孔子说："圣人，我不可能见到了，能见到君子就可以了。"孔子又说："善人，我不可能见到了，能看到有恒心保持品德的人，就可以了。没有却假装有；空虚却假装充实；穷困却假装富裕。这样的人是难以有恒心保持品德的。"

【注释】

1 斯：就，乃，则。
2 亡：同"无"。
3 盈：丰满，充实。
4 约：穷困。泰：宽裕，豪华，奢侈。

【英译文】

The Master (Confucius) said, I cannot hope ever to meet a Divine Sage; the most I can hope for is to meet a true gentleman. I cannot hope ever to meet a faultless man; the most I can hope for is to meet a man of fixed principles. Yet where all around I see Nothing pretending to be Something, Emptiness pretending to be fullness, Penury pretending to be Affluence, even a man of fixed principles will be none too easy to find.

7.27

子钓而不纲[1]，弋不射宿[2]。

【中译文】

孔子钓鱼，只用钓竿，而不用纲；只射飞着的鸟，不射栖息在巢中的鸟。

【注释】

1 纲：本意是提网的大绳。这里指在河流的水面上横着拉一根大绳，上面系有许多鱼钩以钓鱼。

2 弋(yì)：用带绳的箭射鸟，叫“弋”。这种箭箭尾上系的绳，叫“缴(zhuó)”，是用生丝做成的，又细又韧，箭发射出去以后，还能靠绳收回再连续用。宿：指归巢宿窝的鸟。

【英译文】

The Master (Confucius) fished with a line but not with a net; when shooting, he did not aim at a roosting bird.

7.28

子曰：“盖有不知而作之者，我无是也。多闻，择其善者而从之；多见，而识之[1]。知之次也[2]。”

【中译文】

孔子说：“也许有那种无知而凭空造作的人，可我不是这样。多听，选择其中好的跟着来学习；多看，记在心里。这样学而知之，在知识上，仅次于‘生而知之’的人。”

【注释】

1 识(zhì)：记住。

2 知之次也：即“学而知之者，次也”的意思。“次”，即次一等。孔子主张“生而知之者，上也；学而知之者，次也。”参阅《季氏篇第十六》第九章。

【英译文】

The Master (Confucius) said, There may well be those who can do without knowledge; but I am certainly not one of them. To hear much, pick out what is good and follow it, to see much and make note of it, is the lower of the two kinds of knowledge.

7.29

互乡难与言[1]。童子见，门人惑。子曰：“与其进也[2]，不与其退也，唯何甚？人洁己以进，与其洁也，不保其往也[3]。”

【中译文】

互乡的人很难打交道。但互乡的一个少年却受到孔子的接见，弟子们都疑惑不解。孔子说：“我是赞成他进步的，而不是赞成他退步的。何必做得太过分呢？人家现在使自己行为正确以求进步，我是赞许他现在的行为正确，而不管他以往的行为。”

【注释】

1 互乡：地名。究竟是何处，已不可确考。一说，北

宋地理总志《太平寰宇记》所记徐州沛县合乡的故城，即古时“互乡”之地。

2 与：赞许，赞成，肯定。下同。

3 保：守。引申为追究，纠缠。

【英译文】

It was difficult to communicate with people at Hu village. But an uncapped boy presented himself for an interview. The disciples were in two minds about showing him in. But the Master said, In sanctioning his entry here I am sanctioning nothing he may do when he retires. We must not be too particular. If anyone purifies himself in order to come to us, let us accept this purification, We are not responsible for what he does when he goes away.

7.30

子曰：“仁远乎哉？我欲仁，斯仁至矣。”

【中译文】

孔子说：“仁离我们很遥远吗？只要我们想要做到仁，仁就会到来。”

【英译文】

The Master (Confucius) said, Is Goodness indeed so far away? If we really wanted it, we should find that it was at our very side.

7.31

陈司败问[1]：“昭公知礼乎[2]？”孔子曰：“知礼。”孔子退，揖巫马期而进之曰[3]：“吾闻君子不党[4]，君子亦党乎？君取于吴[5]，为同姓，谓之‘吴孟子’[6]。君而知礼，孰不知礼！”巫马期以告。子曰：“丘也幸，苟有过，人必知之。”

【中译文】

陈司败问：“鲁昭公知礼吗？”孔子答道：“知礼。”孔子出来以后，陈司败向巫马期作了个揖，走近他说：“我听说君子是不偏袒别人的，难道君子也偏袒别人吗？鲁君娶了一个吴国女子，是同姓，却称她为‘吴孟子’。如果说鲁君知礼，还有谁不知礼呢？”巫马期把这些话告诉孔子。孔子说：“我真幸运，如果有过错，别人一定会知道。”

【注释】

1 陈司败：陈国的司寇（主管司法的官员）。一说，姓陈，名司败，是齐国大夫。

2 昭公：鲁国国君，姓姬，名裯（chóu），公元前541年至公元前510年在位。“昭”是死后的谥号。

3 揖（yī）：拱手行礼，作揖。巫马期：孔子的弟子，

fact. Now if, as a prince, he is considered to know rites, then who does not know rites?" When Wuma Qi reported this to the Master, the latter said, "I am so lucky! If by any chance I make a mistake, people are certain to know it."

7.32

子与人歌而善，必使反之[1]，而后和之[2]。

【中译文】

孔子同别人一起唱歌，如果别人唱得好，就一定让他再唱一遍，然后自己跟着他唱一遍。

【注释】

1 反：反复，再一次。
2 和(hè)：跟随着唱，应和，唱和。

【英译文】

When in the Master's presence anyone sang a song that he liked, he would asked for it to be repeated and then joined in.

7.33

子曰："文，莫吾犹人也[1]。躬行君子，则吾未之有得。"

【中译文】

孔子说："在文化知识方面，大概我和别人差不多。至于做一个身体力行的君子，我还没有做到。"

姓巫马，名施，字子期。鲁国人。比孔子小三十岁，生于公元前521年，卒年不详。
4 党：偏袒，包庇，有偏私。
5 取：同"娶"。
6 吴孟子：鲁昭公夫人。春秋时，国君夫人的称号，一般是用她出生的国名加上她的姓。吴孟子姓姬，便应称"吴姬"。但是，吴国与鲁国的国君都姓姬(吴是周文王的伯父太伯的后代，鲁国是周文王的儿子周公姬旦的后代)，按照周礼的规定，同姓是不能通婚的。为了掩人耳目，鲁昭公避讳，不称她为"吴姬"，而称"吴孟子"("孟"，指她是长女；"子"，是宋国的姓。一说，"孟子"是昭公夫人的名字，见《左　传·哀公十二年》)。故陈司败批评指责他"君而知礼，孰不知礼"。然而，孔子为什么还说鲁昭公"知礼"呢？这是因为周礼提倡"为尊者讳，为贤者讳，为亲者讳"。孔子宁可自己承担过错，而不说鲁君不知礼。

【英译文】

An official from the Chen State asked whether Duke Zhao of the Lu State knew the rules of propriety. The Master said, "Yes, he does." After the Master had left, the official motioned Wuma Qi to come forward and said, "I have heard that a gentleman is never partial. But it seems that some gentlemen are very partial indeed. Duke Zhao took a woman of Wu as wife, and since she had the same clan name with himself, he called her Wu Mengzi to conceal the

【注释】

1 莫：推测之词。大概，或者，也许。一说，“文莫”连读，即“忞慔”，意为黾（mǐn）勉努力。句中的意思是：在奋勉努力方面，我和别人差不多。

【英译文】

The Master (Confucius) said, As far as taking trouble goes, I do not think I compare badly with other people. But as regards carrying out the duties of a gentleman in actual life, I have never yet had a chance to show what I could do.

7.34

子曰：“若圣与仁，则吾岂敢！抑为之不厌[1]，诲人不倦，则可谓云尔已矣[2]。”公西华曰：“正唯弟子不能学也。”

【中译文】

孔子说：“如果说做到‘圣’与‘仁’，那我怎么敢当！只不过我要朝着‘圣’与‘仁’的方向努力而从不满足，教育别人从不觉得厌倦，对于我尚且可以这样说吧。”公西华说：“这正是弟子学不到的。”

【注释】

1 抑：转折语气词。然则，抑或，或许。

2 云尔：这样，如此。

【英译文】

The Master (Confucius) said, As to being a Divine Sage or even a Good Man, far be it from me to make any such claim. As for unwearying effort to learn and unflagging patience in teaching others, those are merits that I do not hesitate to claim. Gongxi Hua said, The trouble is that we disciples cannot learn!

7.35

子疾病[1]，子路请祷[2]。子曰：“有诸[3]？”子路对曰：“有之。《诔》曰[4]：‘祷尔于上下神祇[5]。’”子曰：“丘之祷久矣[6]。”

【中译文】

孔子病情加重，子路请求祈祷。孔子说：“有这个道理吗？”子路回答说：“有的。《诔》文上说：‘为您向天地上下的神灵祈祷。’”孔子说：“若是这样，我不用祈祷就已经祈祷很久了。”

【注释】

1 疾病：“疾”，就是病。再加一个“病”字，指

病情严重。

2 祷：向鬼神祝告，请求福祐。

3 诸："之乎"的合音。

4 诔(lěi)：一种对死者表示哀悼的文章。这里当作"讄"，指古代为生者向鬼神祈福的祷文。

5 神祇(qí)：古代称天神为"神"，地神为"祇"。

6 "丘之"句："久"，长久。这句话的言外之意：你不必再祈祷了。孔子并不相信向鬼神祈祷能治好病，所以婉言谢绝子路的请求。

【英译文】

When the Master (Confucius) was very ill, Zi Lu asked leave to perform the Rite of Expiation. The Master said, Is there such a thing? Zi Lu answered, There is. In one of the Dirges it says. 'We performed rites of expiation for you, calling upon the sky-spirits above and the earth-spirits below.' The Master said, My expiation began long ago!

7.36

子曰："奢则不孙[1]，俭则固[2]。与其不孙也，宁固。"

【中译文】

孔子说："奢侈了就会不谦逊，节俭了就显得鄙陋，与其不谦逊，不如鄙陋。"

【中译文】

1 孙：同"逊"。恭顺，谦让。

2 固：固陋，鄙陋，小气，寒酸。

【英译文】

The Master (Confucius) said, Just as lavishness leads easily to presumption, so does frugality to meanness. But meanness is a far less serious fault than presumption.

7.37

子曰："君子坦荡荡[1]，小人长戚戚[2]。"

【中译文】

孔子说："君子心胸平坦宽广，小人总是忧愁烦恼。"

【注释】

1 坦：安闲，开朗，直率。荡荡：宽广，辽阔。

2 长：经常，总是。戚戚：忧愁，哀伤，局促不安，患得患失。

【英译文】

The Master (Confucius) said, A true gentleman is calm and at ease; a petty man is fretful and ill at ease.

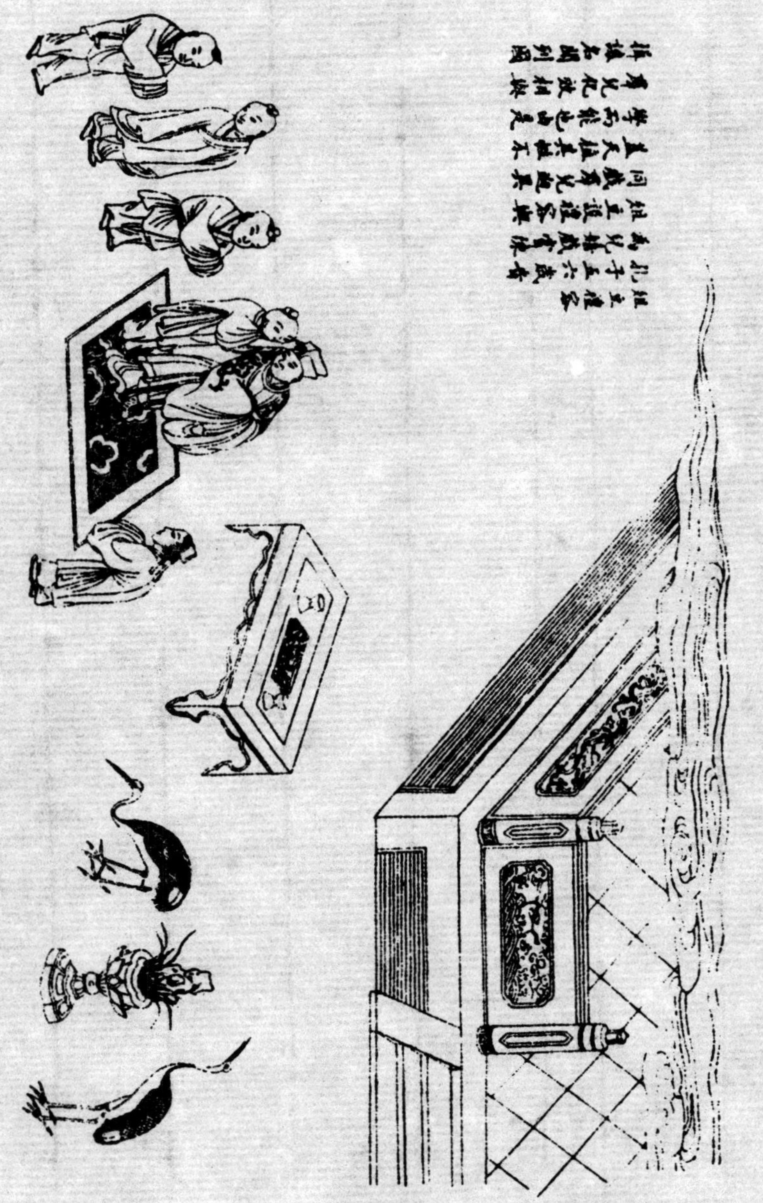

Practicing the Ritual by Displaying Utensils

7.38

子温而厉[1]，威而不猛，恭而安。

【中译文】

孔子温和而又严肃，有威严而不凶猛，恭敬而又安详。

【注释】

1 温：温和。

【英译文】

The Master's (Confucius) manner was affable yet firm, commanding but not harsh, polite but easy.

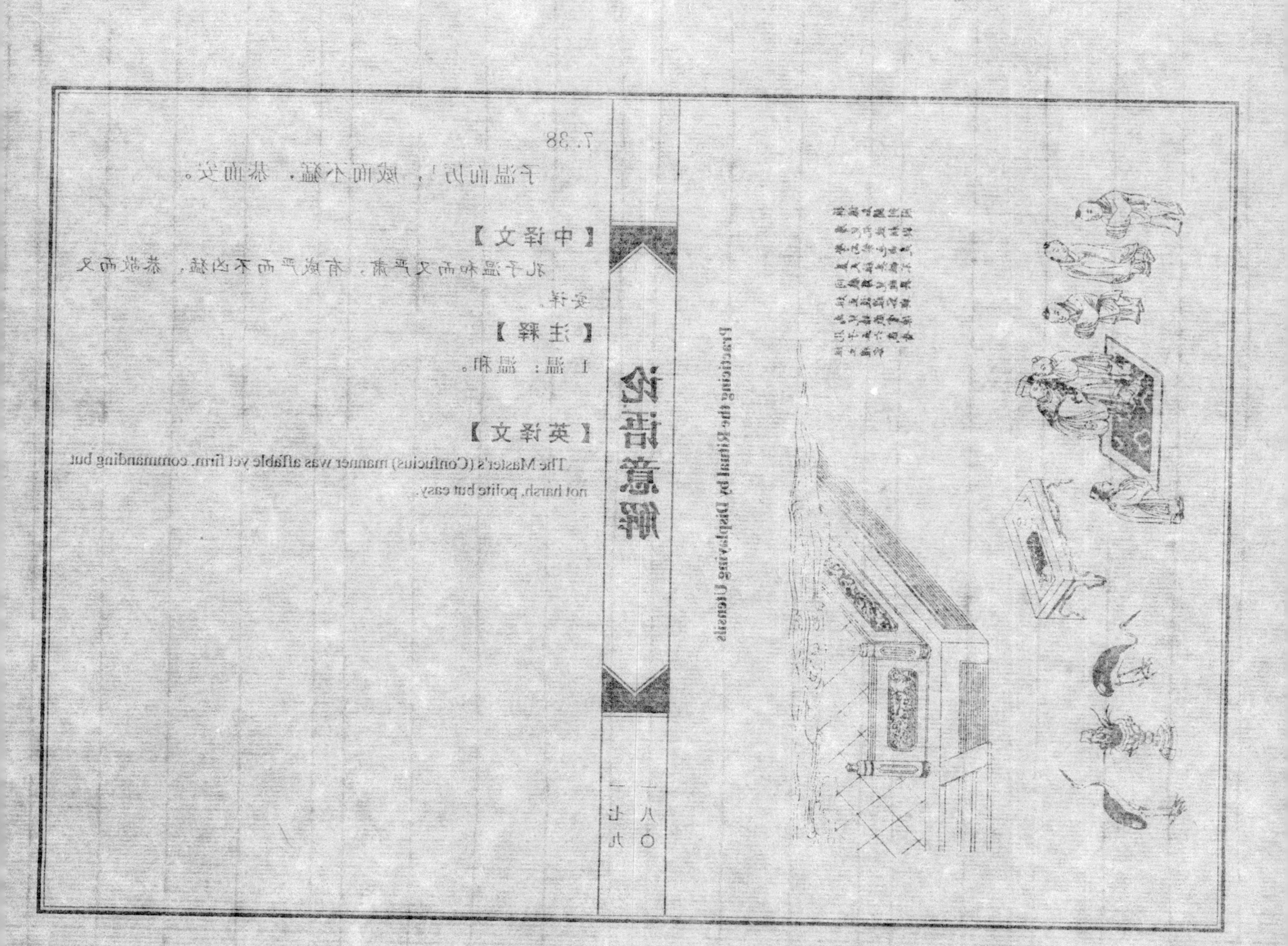

泰伯篇第八（共二十一章）

Confucius and Zengzi Talking the Ancient People

8.1

子曰："泰伯其可谓至德也已矣[1]，三以天下让[2]，民无得而称焉。"

【中译文】

孔子说："泰伯此人可以说是品德最高尚的人了，三次让出国君位置，老百姓虽不了解他的具体事迹，却仍然称颂他。"

【注释】

1 泰伯：周朝姬氏的祖先有名叫古公亶（dǎn）父的，又称"太王"。古公亶父共有三个儿子：长子泰伯（又称"太伯"），次子仲雍，三子季历（即周文王姬昌的父亲）。传说古公亶父见孙儿姬昌德才兼备，日后可成大业，便想把王位传给季历，以谋求后世能扩展基业，有所发展。泰伯体察到了父亲的意愿，就主动把王位的继承权让给三弟季历；而季历则认为，按照惯例，王位应当由长兄继承，自己也不愿接受。后来，泰伯和二弟仲雍密谋，以去衡山采药为名，一起悄悄离开国都，避居于荆蛮地区的勾吴。泰伯后成为周代吴国的始祖。

2 "三以"句："天下"，代指王位。第一次让，是泰伯离开国都，避而出走。第二次让，是泰伯知悉父亲古公亶父去世，故意不返回奔丧，以避免被众臣拥立接受王位。第三次让，是发丧之后，众臣议立新国君时，泰伯在荆蛮地区，索性与当地黎民一样，断发纹身，表示永不返回。这样，他的三弟季历只好继承王位。有了泰伯的这"三让"，才给后来姬昌（周文王）继位统一天下创设了条件，奠定了基础。因此，孔子高度称赞泰伯。

【英译文】

The Master (Confucius) said, Tai Bob can certainly be regarded as a man of virtue. No less than three times he renounced the sovereignty of all things under Heaven, without the people getting a chance to praise him for it.

8.2

子曰："恭而无礼则劳，慎而无礼则葸[1]，勇而无礼则乱，直而无礼则绞[2]。君子笃于亲[3]，则民兴于仁；故旧不遗，则民不偷[4]。"

【中译文】

孔子说："态度恭敬而不讲礼仪就会疲劳；做事谨慎而不讲礼仪就会懦弱；刚强勇猛而不讲礼仪就会作乱；只是直率倔强而不讲礼仪就会说话刻薄。君子如果厚待亲族，老百姓就会崇尚仁德；如果君子不遗弃

怠慢前朝的遗老遗少，老百姓也就厚道了。”

【注释】

1 葸（xǐ）：过分拘谨，胆怯懦弱。

2 绞：说话尖酸刻薄，出口伤人；太急切而不容忍。

3 笃（dǔ）：诚实，厚待。

4 偷：刻薄。

【英译文】

The Master (Confucius) said, Courtesy not bounded by the prescriptions of ritual becomes tiresome. Caution not bounded by the prescriptions of ritual becomes timidity, daring becomes turbulence, inflexibility becomes harshness. The Master said, When gentlemen deal generously with their own kin, the common people are incited to Goodness. When old dependents are not discarded, the common people will not be fickle.

8.3

曾子有疾[1]，召门弟子曰：“启予足[2]，启予手！《诗》云：‘战战兢兢[3]，如临深渊，如履薄冰。’而今而后，吾知免夫。小子[4]！”

【中译文】

曾子病重，召集他的弟子们来，说：“你们看看我的脚，看看我的手。《诗经》中说：‘战战兢兢，好像面临深渊，好像踩上薄冰。’从今以后，我知道如何使自己受之父母的身体会免于毁伤了。弟子们！”

【注释】

1 曾子：曾参，孔子的弟子。《论语》成书时，后世门生记其言行，尊称为“子”。

2 启：看。

3 “战战兢兢”句：引自《诗经·小雅·小旻（mín）》篇。曾参借用这句话，表明自己一生处处小心谨慎，避免身体受损伤，算是尽了孝道。据《孝经》载，孔子曾对曾参说：“身体发肤受之父母，不敢毁伤，孝之始也。”“履”，本义是单底鞋，也泛指鞋。这里作动词用，走，踩，步行。

4 小子：称弟子们。这里说完一番话之后再呼弟子们，表示反复叮咛。

【英译文】

When Zeng Zi was ill he summoned his disciples and said, look at my feet, Look at my hands. The Song says: In fear and trembling, With caution and care, As though on the brink of a chasm, As though treading thin ice. But I feel now that whatever may betide I have got through safely, my disciples.

8.4

曾子有疾，孟敬子问之[1]。曾子言曰：“鸟之将死，其鸣也哀[2]；人之将死，其言也善。君子所贵乎道者三：动容貌[3]，斯远暴慢矣；正颜色，斯近信矣；出辞气[4]，斯远鄙倍矣[5]。笾豆

脚盘。笾和豆都是古代祭祀和典礼中的用具。笾豆之事，就是指祭祀或礼仪方面的事务。

7 有司：古代指主管某一方面事务的官吏。这里具体指管理祭祀或仪礼的小官吏。存：有，存在。

【英译文】

When Zeng Zi was ill, Meng Jingzi came to see him. Zeng Zi spoke to him, When a bird is about to die its song touches the heart. When a man is about to die, his words are of note. There are three things that a gentleman, in following the Way, places above all the rest: from every attitude, every gesture that he employs he must remove all trace of violence or arrogance; every look that he composes in his face must betoken good faith; from every word that he utters, from every intonation, he must remove all trace of coarseness or impropriety. As to the ordering of ritual vessels and the like, there are those whose business it is to attend to such matters.

8.5

曾子曰："以能问于不能，以多问于寡；有若无，实若虚；犯而不校[1]。昔者吾友尝从事于斯矣[2]。"

【中译文】

曾子说："有才能却向没才能的人询问，知识多的却向知识少的人询问；具备却好像缺乏，丰富却好像空虚；别人冒犯也不去计较。从前我的一位朋友就是这样做的。"

之事[6]，则有司存[7]。"

【中译文】

曾子病重，孟敬子去探望他。曾子说："鸟将要死的时候，鸣叫的声音充满悲哀；人将要死的时候，说的话充满善意。君子应当重视这三方面的行为准则：容貌要谦和谨慎，就可以避免粗躁怠慢；脸色要正派庄重，就接近于诚实守信；说话注意言词语气，就可以避免粗野和错谬。至于祭祀和礼节仪式，自有主管的官员去办。"

【注释】

1 孟敬子：姓仲孙，名捷，武伯之子，鲁国大夫。问：看望，探视，问候。

2 也：句中语气助词。表示提顿，以引起下文，兼有舒缓语气的作用。

3 动容貌：即"动容貌以礼"。指容貌谦和，恭敬，从容，严肃，礼貌等。

4 出辞气：即"出辞气以礼"。"出"，是出言，发言。"辞气"，指所用的词句和语气。

5 鄙倍："鄙"，粗野。"倍"，同"背"。指背理，不合理，错误。

6 笾豆之事："笾(biān)"，古代一种竹制的礼器，圆口，下面有高脚，在祭祀宴享时用来盛果脯。"豆"古代一种盛食物盛肉的器皿，木制，有盖，形状像高

【注释】

1 校(jiào)：计较。

2 吾友：我的朋友。

【英译文】

Zeng Zi said, "I once had a friend who was like this: Though capable and gifted, he would inquire of the less capable and gifted; though, he knew much he would inquire of those who knew less; though he was a man of great learning, he acted as if he were ignorant; though he had a rich depth of knowledge, he acted as if he were empty; and he never returned others' mistreatment."

8.6

曾子曰："可以托六尺之孤[1]，可以寄百里之命[2]，临大节而不可夺也[3]。君子人与[4]？君子人也！"

【中译文】

曾子说："可以把年幼的国君托付给他，可以把国家的命运交付给他，面临重大危难有气节而不动摇屈服。这是君子的为人吗？是君子的为人啊！"

【注释】

1 六尺之孤：程树德《论语集释》孔子曰：六尺之孤，幼少之君。

2 寄百里之命："寄"寄托，委托。"百里"，指方圆百里的一个诸侯国。"命"指国家的政权与命运。

3 不可夺：指其志不可夺，不能使他动摇屈服。

4 与：同"欤"。语气词。

【英译文】

Zeng Zi said, The man to whom one could with equal confidence entrust an orphan not yet fully grown or the sovereignty of a whole State, whom the advent of no emergency however great could upset-would such a one be a true gentleman? Surely he is!

8.7

曾子曰："士不可以不弘毅[1]，任重而道远。仁以为己任[2]，不亦重乎？死而后已，不亦远乎？"

【中译文】

曾子说："知识分子不可以不眼光远大、坚韧不拔，他们任重而道远。以己身担当仁义，责任不是很重大吗？要终生为之奋斗到死才停止，时间不也是很长远吗？"

【注释】

1 弘毅："弘"，广大，开阔，宽广。"毅"，坚强，果敢，刚毅。程颢解说："弘而　不毅，

则无规矩而难立；毅而不弘，则隘陋而无以居之。”“弘　大刚毅，然后能胜重任而远到。”

2 “仁以”：把实现仁德看作是自己的任务。

【英译文】

Zeng Zi said, A gentleman must be both broad-shouldered and stout of heart; his burden is heavy and he has far to go. For Goodness is the burden he has taken upon himself; and must we not grant that it is a heavy one to bear? Only with death does his journey end; then must we not grant that he has far to go?

8.8

子曰：“兴于《诗》[1]，立于礼[2]，成于乐[3]。”

【中译文】

孔子说：“君子应当以《诗经》作为培植仁德的引子，以礼作为培植仁德的依据，以乐作为培植仁德的目的。”

【注释】

1 兴：兴起，勃发，激励；受到《诗经》的感染，而热爱真善美，憎恨假恶丑。

2 立：立足于社会，树立道德。

3 成：完成，达到。这里指以音乐来陶冶情操，涵养高尚的人格，完成学业，最终达到全社会“礼乐之治”的最高境界。

【英译文】

The Master (Confucius) said, Let a man be first incited by the Songs, then given a firm footing by the study of ritual, and finally perfected by music.

8.9

子曰：“民可使由之[1]，不可使知之。”

【中译文】

孔子说：“可以让老百姓去做，却很难使他们知道为什么要这么做。”

【注释】

1 由：从，顺从，听从，经由什么道路。孔子认为下层百姓才智能力、认识水平、觉悟程度各不一样，当政者在施行政策法令时，只能要求他们遵照着去做，而不一定使所有人都知道这样做的道理。

【英译文】

The Master (Confucius) said, The common people can be made to follow our intention, they cannot be made to understand it.

8.10

子曰：“好勇疾贫[1]，乱也。人而不仁[2]，疾之已甚[3]，乱也。”

【中译文】

孔子说："那些崇尚武力却不安于贫困的人好作乱。而对不仁之人挤兑太过、也会使他们作乱。"

【注释】

1 疾：厌恶，憎恨。

2 人而不仁：不仁的人。

3 已甚：太过分，很厉害。

【英译文】

The Master (Confucius) said, One who is by nature daring and is suffering from poverty is likely to break the law. Indeed, any men, save those that are truly Good, if their sufferings are very great, will be likely to rebel.

8.11

子曰："如有周公之才之美，使骄且吝[1]，其馀不足观也已。"

【中译文】

孔子说："如果有周公那样智能技艺之美，使之骄傲自大而且吝啬小气的话，那么也就不值得一谈了。"

【注释】

1 吝(lìn)：吝啬，小气，过分爱惜，应当用而不用。

【英译文】

The Master (Confucius) said, If a man has gifts as wonderful as those of Duke Zhou, yet is arrogant and mean, all the rest is of no account.

8.12

子曰："三年学，不至于谷[1]，不易得也。"

【中译文】

孔子说："学了三年，还没有做官的打算，是难得的啊。"

【注释】

1 谷：谷子，小米。古代官吏以谷子来计算俸禄，这里以"谷"代指做官及其俸禄。

【英译文】

The Master (Confucius) said: One who will study for three years Without thought of reward Would be hard indeed to find.

8.13

子曰："笃信好学，守死善道[1]，危邦不入，乱邦不居[2]。天下有道则见[3]，无道则隐。邦有道，贫且贱焉，耻也；邦无道，富且贵焉，耻也。"

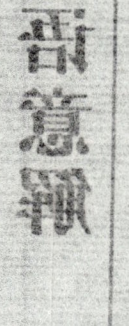

【中译文】

孔子说："坚定信念，爱好学习，至死坚持仁道，不进入有危险的国家；不居住在有祸乱的国家。天下有道，就出来从政；天下无道，就隐居起来。国家有道，贫贱是耻辱；国家无道，富贵是耻辱。"

【注释】

1 道：这里指治国作人的原则与方法。下文"邦有道""邦无道"则指社会政治局面的好与坏，国家政治是否走上正道。

2 危邦，乱邦：东汉儒学家包咸解说："臣弑君，子弑父，乱也；危者，将乱之兆（征兆，预兆）也。"

3 见：同"现"。表现，出现，出来。

【英译文】

The Master (Confucius) said, A man should be of unwavering good faith, love learning, if attacked be ready to die for the good Way. Do not enter a State that pursues dangerous courses, nor stay in one where the people have rebelled. When the Way prevails under Heaven, then show yourself; when it does not prevail, then hide. When the Way prevails in your own land, count it a disgrace to be needy and obscure; when the Way does not prevail in your land, then count it a disgrace to be rich and honoured.

8.14

子曰："不在其位，不谋其政[1]。"

【中译文】

孔子说："不在那个职位上，就不要谋划那方面的政事。"

【注释】

1 谋：参与，考虑，谋划。

【英译文】

The Master (Confucius) said, He who isn't in charge of a State does not discuss its policies.

8.15

子曰："师挚之始[1]，《关雎》之乱[2]，洋洋乎盈耳哉！"

【中译文】

孔子说："从乐师挚演奏开始，到结尾合奏《关雎》，多么美丽博大啊，那充满在我耳朵中的乐曲！"

【注释】

1 师挚之始："师"，指太师，乐师。鲁国的乐师名挚（zhì），一名"乙"。因他擅长弹琴，又称"琴挚"。"始"，乐曲的开端，即序曲。古代奏乐，开端叫"升歌"，一般由太师演奏，故说"师挚之始。"

2 关雎：《诗经》的第一篇。参见前《八佾篇第三》第二十章。乱：乐曲结尾的一段，由多种乐器合

奏。这里指演奏到结尾时所奏的《关雎》乐章。

【英译文】

The Master (Confucius) said, When Zhi the Chief Musician led the climax of Guan Ju, what a grand flood of sound filled one's ears!

8.16

子曰："狂而不直，侗而不愿[1]，悾悾而不信[2]，吾不知之矣。"

【中译文】

孔子说："狂妄而不正直，幼稚无知还不老实，表面上诚恳却不守信用，我不知道这种人怎么会这样。"

【注释】

1 侗(tóng)：幼稚无知。愿：谨慎，老实，厚道。

2 悾悾(kōng)：诚恳。这里指表面上装出诚恳的样子。

【英译文】

The Master (Confucius) said, Impetuous, but tricky! Ingenuous, but dishonest! Simple-minded, but capable of breaking promises! To such men I really don't understand.

8.17

子曰："学如不及，犹恐失之。"

【中译文】

孔子说："学习就像追赶什么而追不上那样，追上了还恐怕再失去它。"

【英译文】

The Master (Confucius) said, Learn as if you were following someone whom you could not catch up with, as though it were someone you were frightened of losing.

8.18

子曰："巍巍乎[1]，舜、禹之有天下也，而不与焉[2]。"

【英译文】

孔子说："多么崇高伟大啊，舜、禹得到了天下，却不以此自是。"

【注释】

1 巍巍：本是形容高大雄伟的山，在这里用，是赞美舜和禹的崇高伟大。

【英译文】

The Master (Confucius) said, Sublime were Shun and Yu! All that is under Heaven was theirs, yet they remained aloof from it.

8.19

子曰："大哉，尧之为君也！巍巍乎，唯天为大，唯尧则之[1]。荡荡乎[2]，民无能名焉[3]。巍巍乎，其有成功也。焕乎[4]，其有文章[5]。"

【中译文】

孔子说："伟大呀，尧作为君主！多么崇高啊，只有天是最高大的，只有尧才能效法天。他的恩德功绩多么广大啊，人民不知该怎样称赞他。多么崇高啊，他成就的功业。多么光辉啊，他制定的礼乐典章制度。"

【注释】

1 则：效法　取法。

2 荡荡：广大，广远，广博无边。

3 名：用言语去形容，赞美。

4 焕：光辉，光明。

5 文章：指礼乐典章制度。

【英译文】

The Master (Confucius) said, Greatest, as lord and ruler, was Yao. Sublime, indeed, was he. 'There is no greatness like the greatness of Heaven', yet Yao could copy it. So boundless was it that the people could find no name for it; yet sublime were his achievements, dazzling the insignia of his culture!

8.20

舜有臣五人[1]，而天下治。武王曰："予有乱臣十人[2]。"孔子曰："才难。不其然乎？唐虞之际[3]，于斯为盛[4]，有妇人焉，九人而已。三分天下有其二[5]，以服事殷。周之德，其可谓至德也已矣。"

【中译文】

舜有贤臣五人，就能把天下治理好。周武王说："我有能治理国家的大臣十人。"孔子说："人才难得。难道不是这样么？在唐尧、虞舜时代之后，周武王时期人才最盛，然而这其中还有一位是妇女，实际上只有九人而已。周文王已经占有了三分之二的天下，他却仍然向殷纣王称臣，周朝的道德，可以说是达到最高境界了。"

【注释】

1 "舜有"句：传说舜有五位贤臣，分别是：禹、稷（jì），契（xiè）、皋陶（gāo yáo），伯益。

2 乱臣十人："乱"在这里是治理的意思。"乱臣"，指能治理国家的大臣。十人是：周公旦，召公奭（shì），太公望，毕公，荣公，太颠，闳夭，散宜生，南宫适（武王曾命他"散鹿台之财，发钜桥之粟，以赈贫弱"。与孔子弟子南宫适不是一人），别有一名妇女是邑姜（南宫适夫人，专管内务）。

而祭祀时却穿华美的礼服；他的住处简陋，却尽力兴修水利，挖沟开辟田间水道。对于禹，我没有可挑剔的地方啊！”

【注释】

1 间(jiàn)：本意指空隙。这里用作动词，含有挑剔、批评、非议等意思。

2 菲(fěi)：菲薄，不丰厚。致：致力，努力去做。

3 黻冕(fǔ miǎn)：祭祀时穿的礼服，叫黻；官职在大夫以上的人戴的礼帽，叫冕。

4 卑：低矮狭小，简陋。洫(xù)：田间的水道，起着正疆界、备旱涝的作用。

【英译文】

The Master (Confucius) said, I can find no fault in Yu. Abstemious in his own food and drink, he displayed the utmost devotion in his offerings to spirits and divinities. Content with the plainest clothes for common wear, he saw to it that his sacrificial apron and ceremonial head-dress were of the utmost magnificence. His place of habitation was of the humblest, and all his energy went into draining and ditching. I can find no fault in Yu.

3 唐虞之际：尧舜之时。“唐”，尧的国号。“虞”，舜的国号。“际”，时期，时候。

4 斯：代词。指周武王时代。

5 “三分”句：传说商纣时天下分为九州，归附文王的已有六个州(荆，梁，雍，豫，徐，扬)，只有青、兖、冀三州属商纣王。

【英译文】

Shun had five ministers and everything under Heaven was well ruled. King Wu said, I have ten ministers. The Master said, True indeed is the saying that 'the right material is hard to find'; for the turn of the Tang and Yu dynasties was the time most famous for this. There was a woman among his ten, so that in reality there were only nine men. Yet of all that is under Heaven he held two parts in three, using them in submissive service to the Yin dynasty. The moral power of Zhou may, indeed, be called an absolutely perfect moral power!

8.21

子曰：“禹，吾无间然矣[1]！菲饮食而致孝乎鬼神[2]；恶衣服而致美乎黻冕[3]；卑宫室而尽力乎沟洫[4]。禹，吾无间然矣！”

【中译文】

孔子说：“对于禹，我没有可挑剔的地方啊。他的饮食菲薄，却以丰盛的祭品孝敬鬼神；他的衣着简朴，

3 唐虞之际：尧舜之时。"唐"，尧的国号。"虞"，舜的国号。"际"，时期，时候。
4 斯：代词。指周武王时代。
5 "三分"句：传说商纣时天下分为九州，归附文王的已有六个州(荆、梁、雍、豫、徐、扬)，只有青、兖、冀三州属商纣王。

【英译文】

Shun had five ministers and everything under Heaven was well ruled. King Wu said, I have ten ministers. The Master said, True indeed is the saying that 'the right material is hard to find'; for the turn of the Tang and Yu dynasties was the time most famous for this. There was a woman among his ten, so that in reality there were only nine men. Yet of all that is under Heaven he held two parts in three, using them in submissive service to the Yin dynasty. The moral power of Zhou may, indeed, be called an absolutely perfect moral power!

8.21

子曰："禹，吾无间然矣[1]！菲饮食而致孝乎鬼神[2]；恶衣服而致美乎黻冕[3]；卑宫室而尽力乎沟洫[4]。禹，吾无间然矣！"

【中译文】

孔子说："对于禹，我没有可挑剔的地方啊。他的饮食菲薄，却以丰盛的祭品孝敬鬼神；他的衣着简朴，而祭祀时却穿华美的礼服；他的住处简陋，却尽力兴修水利，挖沟开渠田间水道。对于禹，我没有可挑剔的地方啊！"

【注释】

1 间(jiàn)：本意指空隙。这里用作动词，含有挑剔、批评、非议等意思。
2 菲(fěi)：菲薄，不丰厚。致：致力，努力去做。
3 黻冕(fú miǎn)：祭祀时穿的礼服，叫黻；官职在大夫以上的人戴的礼帽，叫冕。
4 卑：低矮狭小，简陋。洫(xù)：田间的水道，起着正疆界、备旱涝的作用。

【英译文】

The Master (Confucius) said, I can find no fault in Yu. Abstemious in his own food and drink, he displayed the utmost devotion in his offerings to spirits and divinities. Content with the plainest clothes for common wear, he saw to it that his sacrificial apron and ceremonial head-dress were of the utmost magnificence. His place of habitation was of the humblest, and all his energy went into draining and ditching. I can find no fault in Yu.

子罕篇第九（共三十章）

Encourage People to Study Hard

9.1

子罕言，利[1]，与命，与仁[2]。

【中译文】

孔子很少谈论功利，天命，仁德。

【注释】

1 罕：少。

2 与：是连词“和”。

【英译文】

The Master (Confucius) hardly spoke of profit or fate or Goodness.

9.2

达巷党人曰[1]：“大哉孔子！博学而无所成名。”子闻之，谓门弟子曰：“吾何执[2]？执御乎？执射乎？吾执御矣。”

【中译文】

达巷那个地方的人说：“伟大呀孔子，博学，但却没有可以成名的专长。”孔子听到这话，对学生们说：“我专做什么呢？驾车吗？射箭吗？我从事驾车吧！”

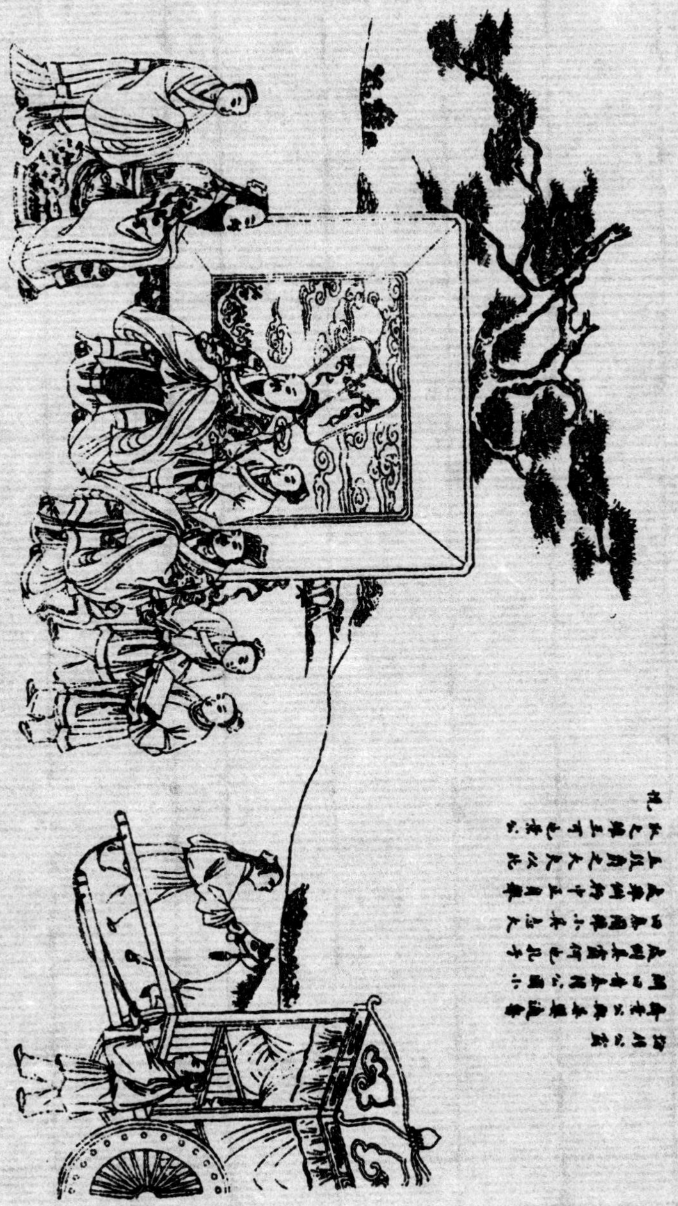

论穆公霸 Discussion of Duke Mugong's Domination

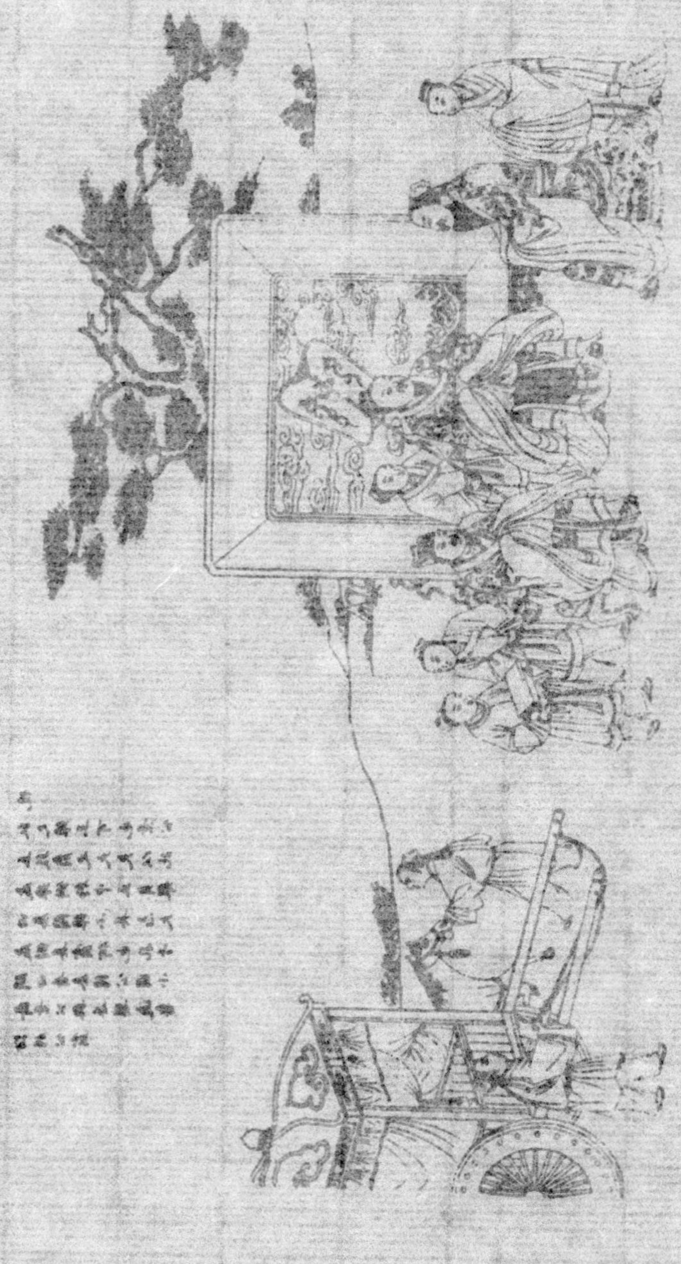

【注释】

1 达巷党人：达巷那个地方的人。“达巷”，地名。山东省滋阳县(今兖州市)西北，相传即达巷党人所居。“党”，古代地方组织，五百家为一党。一说，“达巷党人”，指项橐(tuó)。传说项橐七岁为孔子师。

2 执：专做，专门从事。

【英译文】

A villager from Daxiang said, Confucius is no doubt a very great man and vastly learned. But he does nothing to bear out this reputation. The Master, hearing of it, said to his disciples, What shall I take up? Shall I take up chariot-driving? Or shall it be archery? I think I will take up driving!

9.3

子曰：“麻冕[1]，礼也；今也纯[2]，俭[3]。吾从众。拜下[4]，礼也；今拜乎上，泰也[5]。虽违众，吾从下。”

【中译文】

孔子说：“用麻布做的礼帽，符合古礼；现在用丝绸做，比较节俭。我赞成众人的做法。臣见君王先在堂下行礼，然后升堂再行礼一次，符合古礼；现在臣见君，不先在堂下拜，而是直接升堂时行一次行礼，这是高傲轻慢的表现。虽然有违时下众人的做法，我还

是赞成先在堂下行礼。”

【注释】

1 麻冕：用麻布制成的礼帽。按古时规定，要用两千四百根麻线，织成二尺二寸宽(约合现在一尺五寸)的布来做。很费工，所以不如用丝绸俭省。

2 纯：黑色的丝绸。

3 俭：节俭，俭省。

4 拜下：按照传统古礼，臣见君王，先在堂下跪拜；君王打了招呼之后，到堂上再跪拜一次。

5 泰：轻慢，骄奢。

【英译文】

The Master (Confucius) said, The hemp-thread hat is prescribed by ritual. Nowadays people wear black silk, which is economical; and I follow the general practice. Obeisance at the foot of the court is prescribed by ritual. Nowadays people make obeisance after mounting the stage. This is presumptuous, and though to do so is contrary to the general practice, I make a point of bowing while still down below.

9.4

子绝四：毋意[1]，毋必[2]，毋固[3]，毋我[4]。

【中译文】

孔子杜绝了四种毛病：不凭空猜测假推，不必然绝对，不固执拘泥，不自以为是。

匡地，被围困拘禁。其原因有二：一、当时楚国正进攻卫、陈，当地百姓不了解孔子，对他怀疑，有敌意，有戒心。二、匡地曾遭受鲁国阳货的侵扰暴虐。阳货，又名阳虎（一说，字货），是春秋后斯鲁国季氏的家臣，权势很大。当阳货侵扰匡地时，孔子的一名弟子颜克曾经参与。这 次，孔子来到匡地，正好是颜克驾马赶车，而孔子的相貌又很像阳货，人们认出了颜克，于是以为是仇人阳货来了，便将他包围，拘禁了五天，甚至想杀他。直到弄清真情，才放了他们。

2 文王：周文王。姓姬，名昌，西周开国君王周武王（姬发）的父亲。孔子认为文王是古代圣人之一。

3 兹：这，此。这里指孔子自己。

4 后死者：孔子自称。与：参与。引申为掌握，了解。一说，通“举”。兴起。

5 如予何：把我如何，能把我怎么样。“予”，我。

【英译文】

When the Master was trapped in Kuang, he said, When King Wen perished, did that mean that culture ceased to exist? If Heaven had really intended that such culture as his should disappear, a latter-day mortal would never have been able to link himself to it as I have done. And if Heaven does not intend to destroy such culture, what have I to fear from the people of Kuang?

【注释】

1 毋：同“勿”。不，不要。意：推测，猜想。

2 必：必定，绝对化。

3 固：固执，拘泥。

4 我：自私，自以为是，惟我独尊。

【英译文】

There were four things that the Master was entirely free from: he took nothing for granted, he was never over-positive, never obstinate, never egotistic.

9.5

子畏于匡[1]，曰：“文王既没[2]，文不在兹乎[3]？天之将丧斯文也，后死者不得与于斯文也[4]；天之未丧斯文也，匡人其如予何[5]！”

【中译文】

孔子在匡地受到围困，他说：“周文王已经死了，但周文化我仍掌握着。上天如果想要毁灭这种文化，我就不可能掌握这种文化了；上天如果不毁灭这种文化，匡人又能把我怎么样呢？”

【注释】

1 子畏于匡：“畏”受到威胁，被拘禁。“匡”，地名。今河南省长垣县西南十五里有“匡城”，疑即此地。公元前496年，孔子从卫国去陈国时，经过

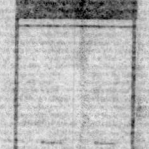

9.6

太宰问于子贡曰[1]："夫子圣者与[2]？何其多能也？"子贡曰："固天纵之将圣[3]，又多能也。"子闻之，曰："太宰知我乎？吾少也贱，故多能鄙事[4]。君子多乎哉？不多也。"

【中译文】

太宰问子贡："孔夫子是位圣人吧？怎么这么多才多艺呢？"子贡说："这是上天使他成为圣人，并使他多才多艺的。"孔子听到后，说："太宰真了解我吗？我少时贫贱，所以会许多卑贱的技艺。君子需要这么多的技艺吗？不需要的啊。"

【注释】

1 太宰：周代掌管国君宫廷事务的官员。当时，吴、宋二国的上大夫，也称太宰。一说，这人就是吴国的太宰伯嚭（pǐ），不可确考。

2 与：同"欤"。语气助词。

3 纵：让，使，听任，不加限量。

4 鄙事：低下卑贱的事。孔子年轻时曾从事农业劳动，放过羊，赶过车，当过仓库保管，还当过司仪，会吹喇叭演奏乐器等等。

【英译文】

The Prime Minister of Wu asked Zi Gong, "Is your Master a sage? Why

does he know so many trades?" Zi Gong replied, "It was Heaven that intended him to become a sage and be able to know many trades." When the Master heard of this, he said, "How should the Prime Minister know me? When I was young I was very poor, so I learned to do many practical things. Does a gentleman possess so many trades? No , he is in no need of them at all."

9.7

牢曰[1]："子云：'吾不试[2]，故艺。'"

【中译文】

牢说："孔子说过：'我没有去做官，所以才学会许多技艺。'"

【注释】

1 牢：有人认为是孔子的弟子琴牢。姓琴，字子开，一字子张，或称"琴张"。卫国人。但《史记·仲尼弟子列传》并无此人。

2 试：用。引申为被任用，做官。

【英译文】

Lao said, our Master used to say, It is because I have not been given a chance that I have become so handy.

9.8

子曰："吾有知乎哉？无知也。有鄙夫问于

我[1]，空空如也。我叩其两端而竭焉[2]。”

【中译文】

孔子说：“我有知识吗？没有。有时乡下人问我问题，我不懂；就从问题的发生与结果，正面与反面等等诸方面去推理，往往能得到一些解答 ”

【注释】

1 鄙夫：这里指乡村的人。“鄙”周制，以五百家为“鄙”。后也称小邑、边邑为“鄙”。

2 叩：询问。两端：两头。指事情(问题)的正反、始终、本末等两个方面。竭：完全，穷尽。

【英译文】

The Master (Confucius) said, Do I regard myself as a possessor of wisdom? Far from it. But if even a simple peasant comes in all sincerity and asks me a question, I am ready to thrash the matter out, with all its pros and cons, to the very end.

9.9

子曰：“凤鸟不至[1]，河不出图[2]，吾已矣夫！”

【中译文】

孔子说：“凤鸟不飞来，黄河也不出瑞祥，我也没

办法了！”

【注释】

1 凤鸟：古代传说中的一种神鸟。雄的叫“凤”雌的叫“凰”，羽毛非常美丽，为百鸟之王。传说凤鸟在舜的时代和周文王时代出现过。凤鸟的出现，象征着天下太平，“圣王”将要出世。

2 图：传说上古伏羲时代，黄河中有龙马背上驮着“八卦图”出现。“图”的出现，是“圣人受命而王”的预兆。《尚书·周书·顾命》篇，记有“河图”之事。文中，孔子以“凤”“图”之说，表示自己对当时政治黑暗，天下混乱，“大道不行” 的失望。

【英译文】

The Master (Confucius) said, The phoenix does not come; the Yellow river gives forth no chart, It is all over with me!

9.10

子见齐衰者[1]，冕衣裳者与瞽者[2]，见之，虽少，必作[3]；过之，必趋[4]。

【中译文】

孔子看见穿丧服的人，戴礼帽穿礼服的人和盲人，即使他们年轻，会见时，孔子也一定站起身来；

从他们面前经过时，也一定要轻轻弯腰走过。

【注释】

1 齐衰（zī cuī）：古代用麻布做的丧服。为五服之一，因其缉边缝齐，故称。“齐”，衣的下摆。

2 冕衣裳者：“冕”，做官人戴的高帽子；“衣”，上衣；“裳”，下服。总起来指穿着礼服（官服）的人。瞽（gǔ）：双目失明，盲人。

3 作：站起身来。表示同情和敬意。

4 趋：迈小步快走。也是表示敬意。

【英译文】

When the Master (Confucius) met a man dressed in the robes of mourning or wearing ceremonial headdress, with gown and skirt, or a blind man, even if such a one were younger than himself, the Master on seeing him invariably rose to his feet, and if compelled to walk past him always quickened his step.

9.11

颜渊喟然叹曰[1]：“仰之弥高[2]，钻之弥坚[3]；瞻之在前[4]，忽焉在后。夫子循循然善诱人[5]，博我以文，约我以礼，欲罢不能，既竭吾才。如有所立卓尔[6] 虽欲从之，末由也已[7]。”

【中译文】

颜渊感叹地说：“老师让人觉得越仰望越觉得高远；越钻研越觉得坚固；前面刚看到后面又忽然显现在后面，老师善于循循诱导，用文化典籍来丰富我的知识，用礼节来约束我，使我想停止前进也不可能，直到竭尽了我的才力去学习。总好像有一个非常高大的东西立在前面，虽然很想要攀登上去，却由不得自己。”

【注释】

1 喟（kuì）：叹气，叹息。

2 弥：更加，越发。

3 钻：深入钻研。坚：本意是坚硬，坚固。这里引申为深，艰深。

4 瞻（zhān）：看，视。

5 循循然：一步一步有次序地。诱：引导，诱导。

6 卓尔：高大直立的样子。

7 末由：指不知从什么地方，不知怎么办，没有办法去达到。“末”，没有，无。“由”，途径。

【英译文】

Yan Hui said with a deep sigh, The more I look up at the Master's doctrine, the higher it soars. The deeper I bore down into it, the harder it becomes. I see it in front; but suddenly it is behind. The Master skilfully lures one on step by step. He has broadened me with culture, restrained me with ritual. Even if I wanted to stop, I could not. Just when I feel that I have exhausted every resource, something seems to rise up, standing out sharp and clear. Yet though I long to pursue it, I can find no way of getting to it at all.

9.12

子疾病[1]，子路使门人为臣[2]。病间[3]，曰："久矣哉，由之行诈也[4]!无臣而为有臣。吾谁欺？欺天乎？且予与其死于臣之手也，无宁死于二三子之手乎[5]？且予纵不得大葬[6]，予死于道路乎？"

【中译文】

孔子病重，子路要学生们去做家臣。后来孔子的病好转一些，便说："很久了，仲由干这种欺骗人的事！没有家臣却要装作有家臣。让我欺骗谁呢？欺骗上天吗？况且，我与其在家臣的照顾下死去，倒不如在弟子你们的照顾下死去。而且，我即使不能以大夫之礼来隆重安葬，难道我会死在路上没人管吗？"

【注释】

1 疾病："疾"，生病。"病"，病重，病危。

2 臣：指家臣。按当时礼法，只有受封的大夫，才有家臣，死后丧事，也是由家臣负责料理。孔子那时已经不做官了，本来没有家臣，但是子路却要安排门人去充当孔子的家臣，这是为了摆一下排场。准备以大夫之礼来安葬孔子。

3 间(jiàn)：本指间隙。这里指疾病好了一些，病势转轻。

4 由：即子路。姓仲名由，子路是字。

5 无宁："无"，发语词，没有意义。"宁"宁可。"无宁"常与"与其"连用，表示选择。"与其"用在放弃的一面，"无宁"用在肯定的一面。二三子：对弟子们的称呼，犹言"你们几位"。

6 大葬：指按葬大夫的礼节来安葬。

【英译文】

When the Master was very ill, Zi Lu had some of his disciples act as his retainers. When the illness eased, the Master said, "For a long time Zhong You has been deceiving me. In pretending to have retainers when I have none, whom do I deceive? Do I deceive Heaven? I would rather die in the hands of you, my disciples, than in the hands of retainers. Even if I would not thus have a grand funeral, shall I die by the roadside?"

9.13

子贡曰："有美玉于斯，韫椟而藏诸[1]？求善贾而沽诸[2]？"子曰："沽之哉！沽之哉！我待贾者也！"

【中译文】

子贡说："有一块美玉在这里，是应该收藏起来呢？还是找一个识货的商人把它卖掉呢？"孔子说："把它卖掉！把它卖掉！我正等着那样的商人哩！"

【注释】

1 韫椟："韫(yùn)"，收藏起来。"椟(dú)"，柜子。后以"韫椟"表示怀才未用。

2 贾(gǔ)：商人。古代称行商，为商；有固定店铺的商人，为贾。沽(gū)：卖，买。诸：“之乎”二字的合音。

【英译文】

Zi Gong said, Suppose one had a lovely jewel, should one wrap it up, put it in a box and keep it, or try to get the best price one can for it? The Master said, Sell it! Most certainly sell it! I myself am one who is waiting for an offer.

9.14

子欲居九夷[1]。或曰：“陋[2]，如之何？”子曰：“君子居之，何陋之有？”

【中译文】

孔子想要迁到九夷地方居住。有人说：“那里很僻陋，怎么能居住呢？”孔子说：“君子居住到那里，还有什么僻陋的呢？”

【注释】

1 九夷：我国古代称东部的少数民族为夷。至于“九夷”，或说是指九个不同的部族；或说是对东部夷族地区的总称；或说即“淮夷”，是散居于淮水、泗水之间的一个部族。已不可确考。

2 陋：本义是狭小，简陋。这里引申为经济、文化的落后。

【英译文】

The Master (Confucius) wanted to settle among the Nine Wild Tribes of the East. Someone said, I am afraid you would find it hard to put up with their lack of refinement. The Master said, Were a true gentleman to settle among them there would soon be no problem about lack of refinement.

9.15

子曰：“吾自卫反鲁[1]，然后乐正，《雅》《颂》各得其所[2]。”

【中译文】

孔子说：“我自卫国返回鲁国，音乐就得到了规范，雅归雅，颂归颂，各归于适当的位置。”

【注释】

1 自卫反鲁：“反”，同“返”。指公元前484年(鲁哀公十一年)冬，因卫国发生内乱，孔子从那儿返回鲁国，结束了他十四年来“周游列国”的生活。

2 雅，颂：《诗经》篇章分《风》、《雅》、《颂》三大类。在古代，《诗经》305篇诗，都是能唱的。不同的诗配有不同的乐曲。奏于朝曰雅，奏于庙曰颂。这里指《雅》、《颂》的乐章内容和曲谱，都得到了孔子的整理与订正，而教授弟子，传之于世。

【英译文】

The Master (Confucius) said, It was only after my return from Wei to Lu

that music was revised, Court pieces and Ancestral Recitations being sorted and given their proper places.

9.16

子曰："出则事公卿，入则事父兄，丧事不敢不勉，不为酒困，何有于我哉[1]？"

【中译文】

孔子说："出外事奉君王公卿，在家侍奉父母兄长，办理丧事不敢不勤勉尽力，不嗜酒贪杯，我做到了哪些呢？"

【注释】

1"何有"句：一说，此句意为：我还有什么困难或遗憾呢？

【英译文】

The Master (Confucius) said, at Court I can claim that I have duly served the Duke and his officers; at home, my father and elder brother. As regards matters of mourning, I am conscious of no neglect, nor have I ever been overcome with wine. Concerning these things at any rate my mind is quite at rest.

9.17

子在川上曰："逝者如斯夫[1]，不舍昼夜[2]。"

【中译文】

孔子站在河边说："逝去的就像这河水一样啊！日日夜夜不停地向前奔流。"

【注释】

1 逝者：指过去的事物和情景。斯：这。这里指河水。夫(fú)：语气助词。

2 舍：止，停留。

【英译文】

Standing by a stream, the Master said, Time goes on and on like this, never ceasing day or night!

9.18

子曰："吾未见好德如好色者也[1]。"

【中译文】

孔子说："我没见过爱慕德行像爱慕美色那样的人。"

【注释】

1"吾未见"句：据《史记·孔子世家》记载，孔子"居卫月馀，灵公与夫人（南子）同车，宦者雍渠参乘出，使孔子为次乘(后面的第二部车子)，招摇市过"之"。孔子因而发出了这一感叹。

【英译文】

The Master (Confucius) said, I have never yet seen anyone whose desire to build up his moral power was as strong as sexual desire.

9.19

子曰："譬如为山，未成一篑[1]，止，吾止也。譬如平地，虽覆一篑[2]，进，吾往也[3]。"

【中译文】

孔子说："比如用土来堆一座山，只差一筐土便能堆成，可是需要停止时，我就自己停止。比如在平地上堆土成山，虽然才倒下一筐土，可是需要继续前进，那我也坚持往前。"

【注释】

1 篑(kuì)：装土用的竹筐子。

2 覆：底朝上翻过来倾倒。

3 往：犹言前进。旧注大多认为本句意为勉励人自强不息，其实是孔子认为应当止于所当止，行其所当行，不因外在客观条件牵制自己的想法。有些时候，虽临近于成功需要停止时虽然可惜，但仍能停止。有些时候，虽然成功希望渺茫，但如有必要，也要知其不可而为之，启动艰难的第一步。

【英译文】

The Master (Confucius) said, "Though in making a mound I shall stop working when only one basketful of earth would finish it, it is because I want to stop. On the other hand, if in leveling land I will go on after throwing down only one basketful of earth, it is because I want to proceed."

9.20

子曰："语之而不惰者[1]，其回也与[2]！"

【中译文】

孔子说："听我对他说话而不懈怠的，大概只有颜回吧！"

【注释】

1 惰：懈怠，不恭敬。

2 其：表示揣测、反诘。莫非，难道，也许。与：同"欤"。语气助词。

【英译文】

The Master (Confucius) said, It was Yan Hui whom I could count on always to listen attentively to anything I said.

9.21

子谓颜渊曰："惜乎！吾见其进也，未见其止也。"

【中译文】

孔子谈到颜渊时说："真值得惋惜追思呀！我只看到他不断前进，从来没见他停止过。"

【英译文】

The Master (Confucius) said of Yan Hui, What a pity that, I saw him go forward. I saw him make progress and never saw him stand still.

9.22

子曰："苗而不秀者有矣夫！秀而不实者有矣夫！"

【中译文】

孔子说："种庄稼只是出苗而不秀穗的是有的吧！只秀穗却不结果实的也是有的吧！"

【英译文】

The Master (Confucius) said, There are shoots whose lot it is to spring up but never to flower; others whose lot it is to flower, but never bear fruit.

9.23

子曰："后生可畏，焉知来者之不如今也？四十、五十而无闻焉，斯亦不足畏也已。"

【中译文】

孔子说："年轻人是值得敬畏的，怎么能认为后来者不居上呢？但如果到了四十岁、五十岁还无所成名，那也就不值得敬畏了。"

【英译文】

The Master (Confucius) said, Respect the young. How do you know that they will not one day be all that you are now? But if a man has reached forty or fifty and nothing has been heard of him, then I grant there is no need to respect him.

9.24

子曰："法语之言[1]，能无从乎？改之为贵。巽与之言[2]，能无说乎[3]？绎之为贵[4]。说而不绎，从而不改，吾末如之何也已矣。"

【中译文】

孔子说："符合礼制规矩的话，能不听从吗？但只有按之改正自己的错误，才是可贵的。顺耳好听的话，能不让人高兴吗？但只有分析鉴别这些话的源头，才是可贵的。如果只高兴而不分析，只听从而不改正自己，对于这样的人我实在没有什么办法啊。"

【注释】

1 法语之言：指符合礼法规范、符合国家法令的正确的话。"法"，法则，规则，原则。

2 巽与之言：“巽(xùn)”，通“逊”，谦逊，恭顺。“与”，赞许，称赞。巽与之言，指那种顺耳好听的、恭维称道的言词。

3 说：同“悦”。

4 绎(yì)：本义是抽丝。引申为寻究事理，分析鉴别以便判断真假是非。

【英译文】

The Master (Confucius) said, Correct words cannot fail to stir us; but what matters is that they should change our ways. Flattering words cannot fail to commend themselves to us; but what matters is that we should carry them out. For those who approve but do not carry out, who are stirred, but do not change, I can do nothing at all.

9.25

子曰：“主忠信。毋友不如己者。过则勿惮改[1]。”

【中译文】

孔子说：“做人，主要讲求忠诚，守信用。不要同德行不如自己的人交朋友。有过错，就不要怕改正。”

【注释】

1《学而篇第一》第八章文字与此略同，可参阅。

【英译文】

The Master (Confucius) said, First and foremost, be faithful to your superiors, keep all promises, refuse the friendship of all who are not like you; and if you have made a mistake, do not be afraid of admitting the fact and amending your ways.

9.26

子曰：“三军可夺帅也[1]，匹夫不可夺志也[2]。”

【中译文】

孔子说：“军队可以丧失它的主帅，一个人却不可以丧失他的志向。”

【注释】

1 三军：古制，一万二千五百人为一军。周朝，一个大诸侯国可拥有三军(三万七千五百人)。

2 匹夫：普通的人，男子汉。

【英译文】

The Master (Confucius) said, You may rob the Three Armies of their commander-in-chief, but you cannot deprive the humblest peasant of his opinion.

9.27

子曰：“衣敝缊袍[1]，与衣狐貉者立[2]，而不耻者，其由也与？‘不忮不求，何用不臧[3]？’”子路终身诵之。子曰：“是道也，何足以臧？”

【中译文】

孔子说：“穿着破旧的棉袍，同穿着狐貉皮袍子的人站在一起，而不觉得自己耻辱的人，也许只有仲由吧？《诗经》上说：‘不嫉妒别人，不贪求财物，还有什么不好呢？’”子路经常背诵这两句诗。孔子说：“做到这样固然是道之所在，但还算不上十足的好？”

【注释】

1 衣敝缊袍：“衣”，做动词用，穿。“敝”，破，坏。“缊(yùn)”：乱麻、旧绵絮。全句指穿着破旧的用乱麻掺旧绵絮做的袍子。

2 衣狐貉者：穿着狐狸皮貉皮袍子的人。指富贵者。“貉(hé)”，似狸，毛皮珍贵。

3 “不忮”二句：出自《诗经·邶风·雄雉》篇。“忮(zhì)”，嫉妒别人。“求”，贪求财物。“何用”，何行，什么行为。“臧(zāng)”，好，善。

【英译文】

The Master (Confucius) said, "Zhong You is the only person who wears a shabby silk-quilted gown and yet is capable of standing unabashed among those who wear furs. As it says in The Book of Poetry, 'He does not envy, nor does he seek anything. Why is it not good?' " When Zi Lu kept on chanting those lines to himself, the Master said, "How can it be said good enough if you keep on doing such only?"

9.28

子曰：“岁寒，然后知松柏之后凋也[1]。”

【中译文】

孔子说：“到了寒冷的时节，才知道松柏树是不凋谢的。”

【注释】

1 凋(diāo)：凋零，萎谢，草木花叶脱落。松柏树四季常青，经冬不凋。孔子以此为喻，有“烈火见真金”、“路遥知马力”、“国乱识忠臣”、“士穷显节义”的含意。

【英译文】

The Master (Confucius) said, Only when the year grows cold do we see that the pine and cypress are the last to fade.

9.29

子曰：“知者不惑[1]，仁者不忧，勇者不惧。”

【中译文】

孔子说：“有智慧的人不迷惑，有仁德的人不忧愁，有勇气的人不畏惧。”

【注释】

1 知：同“智”。智，仁，勇，不仅是孔子所提倡

的三种传统美德，而且表明了智慧、仁德与勇气给人生带来的意义与利益。

【英译文】

The Master (Confucius) said, He who is really Good can never be unhappy. He who is really wise can never be perplexed. He that is really brave is never afraid.

9.30

子曰："可与共学，未可与适道[1]；可与适道，未可与立；可与立，未可与权[2]。

【中译文】

孔子说："能够一起学习的人，未必能一起实践；能够一起实践的人，未必能一起坚持下去；能够一起坚持的人，未必能灵活运用，随机应变。

【注释】

1 适：往。这里含有达到、学到的意思。道：指真理。

2 权：本义是秤锤。引申为权衡，随宜而变。

【英译文】

The Master (Confucius) said, There are some whom one can join in study but whom one cannot join in progress along the Way; others whom one can join in progress along the Way, but beside whom one cannot take one's stand; and others again beside whom one can take one's stand, but whom one cannot

join in counsel.

9.31

"唐棣之华，偏其反而。岂不尔思，室是远而[1]。"子曰："未之思也，夫何远之有？"

【中译文】

古诗说："唐棣树的花，摇摇摆摆，先开后合。难道我不思念你吗？你居住得太遥远了。"孔子又说："这是没有真正思念啊，如果真在思念那还有什么遥远不遥远呢？"

【注释】

1 "康棣"四句：古诗。"唐棣(dì)"，又作"棠棣"，"常棣"，树木名。生江南山谷中，一名杉，也叫郁李，属蔷薇科，落叶灌木。《诗经·小雅·常棣》有句："常棣之华，鄂不韡"。大意说，常棣树上的花啊，花萼光明，鲜鲜亮亮。其内含是借棠棣的花与萼相依相托，比喻兄弟的亲密关系与互相友爱。"华"，同"花"。"偏其反而"，此言唐棣之花在风中翩飞翻舞。"偏"，同"翩"。疾飞，随风翻动摇摆。"反"，通"翻"。翻动。"而"，语助词，没有实际意义。"岂不尔思"，即"岂不思尔"。"尔"你。"室"，居住之处。

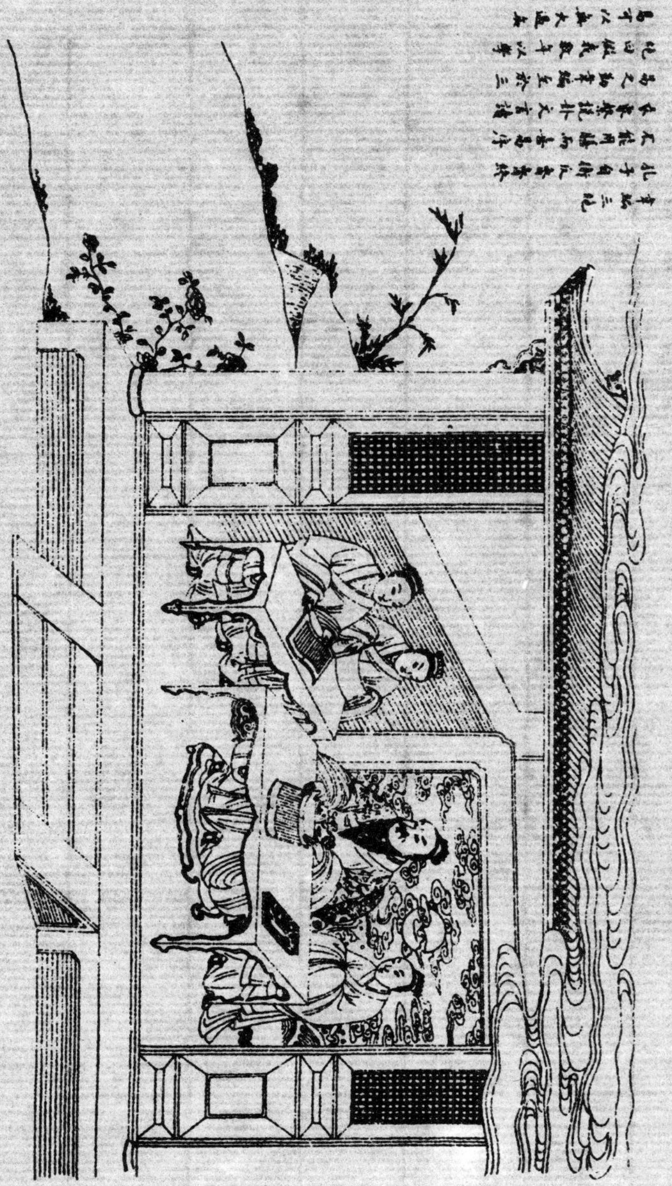

韦编三绝 Reading the Changes Many Times to Make the Rope Break

【英译文】

The flowery branch of the wild cherry How swiftly it flies back! It is not that I do not love you; But your house is far away. The Master said, He did not really love her. Had he done so, he would not have worried about the distance.

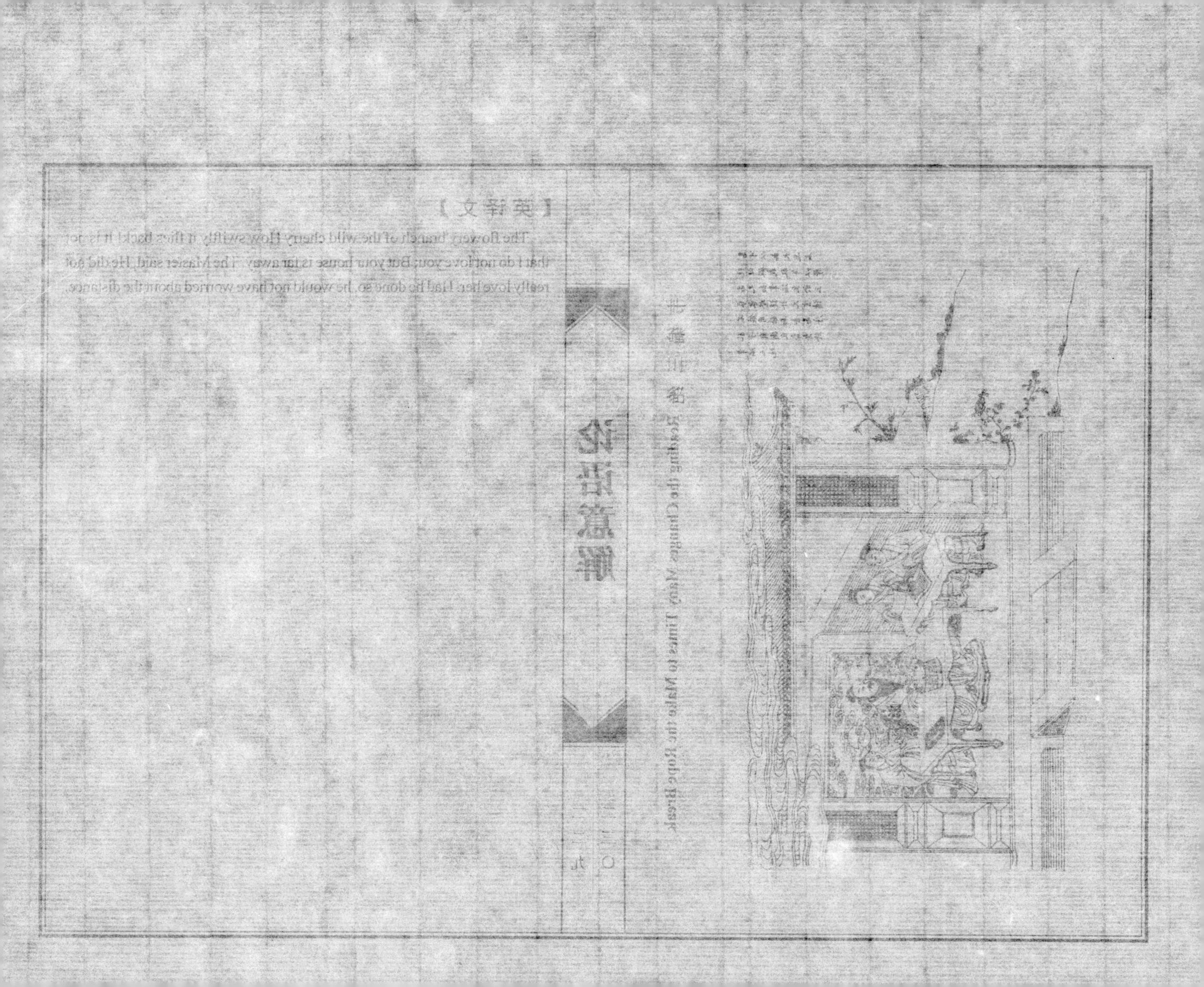

乡党篇第十（共二十七章）

On the Habit of Confucius

10.1

孔子于乡党[1]，恂恂如也[2]。似不能言者。其在宗庙朝廷，便便言[3]，唯谨尔。

【中译文】

孔子在乡人面前表现得十分温和恭顺，似乎不太善于讲话。但是在宗庙祭祀、上朝晋见的场合，他便显得善于言谈，辩论机智，只是比较谨慎罢了。

【注释】

1 乡党：指在家乡本地。古代，一万二千五百户为一乡，五百户为一党。

2 恂恂(xún)：信实谦卑，温和恭顺，而又郑重谨慎的样子。

3 便便(pián)：擅长谈论，善辩。

【英译文】

In his native village, the Master was gentle and respectful, as though he did not trust himself to speak. But in the ancestral temple and at Court he speaks readily, though always choosing his words with care.

10.2

朝，与下大夫言[1]，侃侃如也[2]；与上大夫言，訚訚如也[3]。君在，踧踖如也[4]，与与如也[5]。

【中译文】

孔子在朝廷上，与下大夫说话，温和快乐，从容不迫；与上大夫说话，和颜悦色，恭敬诚恳。君王临朝到来，孔子表现出恭敬而又不安，慢步行走而又小心谨慎。

【注释】

1 下大夫：周代，诸侯以下是大夫。大夫的最高一级，称“卿”，即“上大夫”；地位低于上大夫的，称“下大夫”。孔子当时的地位，属下大夫。

2 侃侃(kǎn)：说话时刚直和乐，理直气壮，而又从容不迫。

3 訚訚(yín)：和颜悦色，而能中正诚恳，直言相诤。

4 踧踖(cù jí)：恭敬而又不安的样子。

5 与与：慢步行步，非常小心谨慎的样子。

【英译文】

At Court when conversing with the Under Ministers, the Master's attitude is friendly and affable; when conversing with the Upper Ministers, it is restrained and formal. When the ruler is present it is wary, but not cramped.

10.3

君召使摈[1]，色勃如也[2]，足躩如也[3]。揖所与立，左右手，衣前后，襜如也[4]。趋进，翼如也[5]。宾退，必复命曰：“宾不顾矣[6]。”

【中译文】

国君命令接待外宾，孔子神情立刻庄重起来，脚步加快。孔子向同他站在一起的人作揖时，左右拱手，衣服前后飘动，都很整齐。快步向前时，他的姿态像鸟儿展翅飞翔。宾客走了以后，一定向国君汇报说：“宾客已经走远了。”

【注释】

1 摈（bìn）：同“傧”。古代称接引招待宾客的负责官员。这里用作动词，指国君下令，使孔子去接待外宾。

2 勃如：心情兴奋紧张，脸面表现得庄重矜持。

3 躩（jué）：快步前进，脚旋转而表敬意。

4 襜（chān）：衣服整齐飘动。

5 翼如：像鸟儿张开翅膀。

6 不顾：不回头看。指客人已走远了。

【英译文】

When the ruler summons the Master to receive a guest, a look of confusion comes over his face and his legs seem to give beneath his weight. When saluting his colleagues he passes his right hand to the left, letting his robe hang down in front and behind; and as he advances with quickened step, his attitude is one of majestic dignity. When the guest has gone, he reports the close of the visit, saying, 'The guest is no longer looking back.'

10.4

入公门，鞠躬如也[1]，如不容。

立不中门，行不履阈[2]。

过位[3]，色勃如也，足躩如也，其言似不足者[4]。

摄齐升堂[5]，鞠躬如也，屏气似不息者[6]。

出，降一等[7]，逞颜色[8]，怡怡如也[9]。

没阶[10]，趋进，翼如也。

复其位，踧踖如也。

【中译文】

孔子走入国君的大厅，低头弯腰非常恭敬，似乎不容他直立进去。站立时不在门的中间，行走时不踩门坎。经过国君的席位时，脸色立刻庄重起来，脚步加快，说话时好像气力不足的样子。提起衣服的下摆向大堂上走的时候，低头弯腰恭敬谨慎，憋住一口气好像没有呼吸一样。出来时，走下一级台阶，才舒展脸色，显出轻松的样子。走完了台阶，快步向前，姿态像鸟儿展翅。回到自己的位置上，还要表现出恭敬而

又不安的样子。

【注 释】

1 鞠躬：这里指低头躬身恭敬而谨慎的样子。

2 履：走，踩。阈（yù）：门限，门槛。

3 过位：按照古代礼节，君王上朝与群臣相见时，前殿正中门屏之间的位置是君王所立之位。到议论政事进入内殿时，群臣都要经过前殿君王所立的位子，这时君王并不在，只是一个虚位，但大夫们“过位”时，为了尊重君位，态度仍必须恭敬严肃。

4 言似不足：说话时声音低微，好像气力不足的样子。一说，同朝者要尽量少说话，不得不应对，也要答而不详，言似不足。这都是为了表示恭敬。

5 摄齐：“摄”，提起，抠起。“齐（zī）”，衣服的下襟，下摆，下缝。朝臣升堂时，一般要双手提起官服的下襟，离地一尺左右，以恐前后踩着衣襟或倾跌失礼。

6 屏气：“屏（bǐng）”，抑制，强忍住。屏气，就是憋住一口气。息：呼吸。

7 降一等：从台阶走下一级。

8 逞颜色：这里指舒展开脸色，放松一口气。“逞”，快意，称心，放纵。

9 怡怡如：轻松愉快的样子。

10 没阶：指走完了台阶。“没（mò）”，尽，终。

【英译文】

On entering the Palace Gate the Master seems to shrink into himself, as if there were not room. If he halts, it must never be in the middle of the gate, nor in going through does he ever tread on the threshold. As he passes the Stance a look of confusion comes over his face, his legs seem to give way under him and words seem to fail him. While, holding up the hem of his skirt. He ascends the Audience Hall, he seems to double up and keeps in his breath, so that you would think he was not breathing at all.

10.5

执圭[1]，鞠躬如也，如不胜[2]。上如揖，下如授。勃如战色，足蹜蹜[3]，如有循[4]。

享礼[5]，有容色。

私觌[6]，愉愉如也[7]。

【中译文】

孔子举着圭的时候，低头弯腰非常恭敬，好像举不动的样子。向上举好像作揖，放下来好像要传递给别人。脸色庄重而昂奋，好像战战兢兢；步子迈得又小又快，好像沿着一条直线往前走。在赠送礼品的仪式上，显出和颜悦色。以个人身份私下会见时，面色轻松自在。

【注 释】

1 圭（guī）：一种上圆下方的长条形玉器。举行朝聘、祭祀、丧葬等礼仪大典时，帝王、诸侯、大夫手里都

必有寝衣，长一身有半。

狐貉之厚以居[10]。

去丧，无所不佩。

非帷裳[11]，必杀之[12]。

羔裘玄冠不以吊[13]。

吉月[14]，必朝服而朝。

【中译文】

君子不用深青透红或黑中透红的布镶边，不用红色或紫色的布做在家穿的便服。夏天，穿粗麻或细麻布做的单衣，但一定要套在外面。冬天，黑色罩衣，配黑羊羔皮袍；白色罩衣，配白鹿皮袍；黄色罩衣，配狐狸皮袍。平常在家穿的皮袍，要做得长一些，右边的袖子短一些。必须有睡衣，要一身半长。要用毛长的狐貉皮制作坐垫。服丧期满脱去丧服，可以佩戴各种装饰品。如果不是礼服，必须加以剪裁，去掉多余的布。不要穿黑羊羔皮袍戴黑色礼帽去吊丧。每月的初一，一定要穿朝服去朝拜。

【注释】

1 绀(gàn)：深青透红(带红)的颜色(一说，天青色)。是古时斋戒服装所用的颜色。緅(zōu)：黑中透红的颜色(一说，铁灰色)。是古时丧服所用的颜色。饰：服装上的装饰。这里指衣服领子、袖子上的镶边等。

要拿着这种玉器。依不同的地位身份，所拿的圭也各有不同。这里指大夫出使到别的诸侯国去，手里拿着代表本国君主的圭，作为信物。

2 不胜：担当不起，承受不住，几乎不能做到。

3 踧踧(sù)：形容脚步细碎紧密，一种小步快走的样子。

4 循：顺着，沿着。

5 享礼：向对方贡献礼品的仪式。“享”，献。

6 觌(dí)：见面，会见，以礼相见。

7 愉愉：快乐，心情舒畅，露出笑容。

【英译文】

When carrying the tablet of jade, The Master seems to double up, as though borne down by its weight. He holds it at the highest as though he were making a bow, at the lowest, as though he were proffering a gift. His expression, too, changes to one of dread and his feet seem to recoil, as though he were avoiding something. When presenting ritual-presents, his expression is placid. At the private audience he looked cheerful.

10.6

君子不以绀緅饰[1]，红紫不以为亵服[2]。

当暑，袗絺绤[3]，必表而出之[4]。

缁衣[5]，羔裘[6]；　素衣[7]，麑裘[8]；黄衣，狐裘。

亵裘长，短右袂[9]。

14 吉月：阴历每月的初一。也称作朔月。一说，只指每年正月岁首。

【英译文】

A gentleman does not wear facings of purple or mauve, nor does he use red or violet at home. In summer he wears an unlined gown of fine or coarse hemp, but puts on an outside garment before going out of doors. Over lambskin he wears black; over fawn's fur he wears white, over fox-skin he wears yellow. At home he wears a long fur robe, with the right sleeve short (for convenience in using the arm). When sleeping he always covers himself with a quilt which is longer than his height. The thick furs of the fox or badger are for cushions. When out of mourning he wears all his girdle-ornaments. Apart from the gown worn at sacrifices and at court, his clothes are always cut and fitted. On visits of condolence, he wears neither black lambskin nor a black hat. On the first day of the year he must go to court in full court dress.

10.7

齐[1]，必有明衣[2]，布。

齐必变食[3]，居必迁坐[4]。

【中译文】

斋戒时，一定要有浴衣，须用布做的。斋戒时，一定要改变饮食习惯，住处一定要从卧室迁出。

【注释】

1 齐：同“斋”。斋戒。

2 亵(xiè)服：平常在家穿的私服、便服。贴身穿的内衣也称亵服。因为红紫色是制做礼服的庄重的颜色，所以，亵服不能用红紫色。

3 袗絺绤：“袗(zhěn)”，单衣。“絺(chī)”，细麻布，葛布。“绤(xì)”粗麻布。袗絺绤，指穿细麻布或粗麻布做的单衣。

4 “必表”句：一定把麻布单衣穿在外表，而里面还要衬上内衣。一说，“表”，是上衣，是套在外表的衣服。古人不论冬夏，出门时都要外加上衣。

5 缁(zī)黑色。

6 羔裘：黑色羊羔皮做的皮袍。

7 素：白色。

8 麑裘：指用小鹿皮做的皮袍。“麑(ní)”，白色幼鹿。

9 短右袂：指右手的袖子做得短一些，便于做事。“袂(mèi)”袖子。

10 “狐貉”句：用厚毛的狐貉皮制做成坐垫。“以”，用。“居”，坐。

11 帷裳：朝拜和祭祀时穿的礼服。古时规定，要用整幅的布来做礼服，多余的布不裁掉，而要折叠起来缝上。

12 杀：消除。这里指剪裁掉。如果不是制做礼服，必须加以剪裁，去掉多馀的布。

13 玄冠：黑色的礼帽。

2 明衣：指斋戒期间沐浴后所换穿的贴身衣服。
3 变食：改变平常的饮食。特指不饮酒，不吃荤，不吃葱蒜韭等有异味的东西。
4 居必迁坐：指斋戒时的住处，要从内室（平时的卧室）迁到外室，不与妻妾同房。

【英译文】

On days of fasting, he always wears a bathrode made of linen cloth, and he changes his food and the place where he usually sleeps.

10.8

食不厌精[1]，脍不厌细[2]。

食饐而餲[3]，鲁馁而肉败[4]，

不食。色恶，不食。臭恶，不食。失饪[5]，不食。不时[6]，不食。割不正，不食。不得其酱，不食。

肉虽多，不使胜食气[7]。

唯酒无量，不及乱[8]。

沽酒市脯[9]，不食。

不撤姜食。不多食[10]。

【中译文】

饭食不嫌做得精，鱼肉不嫌切得细。粮食变质了，

鱼、肉腐烂了，不吃。食物的颜色变坏了，不吃。气味难闻了，不吃。烹煮得不得当，不吃。不到时间，不吃。宰割方法不规矩的肉，不吃。酱、醋作料放得不适当，不吃。肉虽然多，吃时不要超过主食的数量。虽然酒无限量，但不能喝到昏醉的地步。买来的酒和市上的熟肉干，不吃。不去掉姜。不要多吃。

【注 释】

1 不厌：不厌烦，不排斥，不以为不对。
2 脍（kuài）：细切的鱼肉。
3 饐（yì）：食物长久存放，陈旧了，霉烂变质了。餲（ài）：食物放久变了味，馊了。
4 馁（něi）：鱼类不新鲜了，腐烂了。败：肉类不新鲜了，腐烂了。
5 饪（rèn）：烹调，煮熟。
6 不时：不到该吃的时候。指吃饭要定时。一说，不吃过了时的、不新鲜的蔬菜。另说，不到成熟期的粮食、果、菜，不能吃，吃了会伤人。
7 气：同“饩（xì）”。粮食。
8 不及乱：不到喝醉而神智昏乱的地步。
9 脯（fǔ）：熟肉干，干肉。
10 不多食：不多吃，不要吃得过饱而伤肠胃。另说，与“不撤姜食”相连，指每餐都要吃点姜，但也不要多吃姜。

【英译文】

There is no objection to his staple food being of the finest quality, nor to his meat being finely minced. He does not eat rice affected by the weather or turned, nor fish that is not sound. He does not eat anything discolored or that smells bad. He does not eat what is overcooked or what is undercooked, nor does he eat between meals. He does not eat what has not been properly cut, nor any sauce or vinegar that lacks its proper seasoning. Although meat may be abundant, he does not eat more of it than he does of staple food. As regards wine, no limit is laid down, but he does not drink wine or eat cooked meat bought at a shop. He does not refuse food seasoned with ginger, but he does not eat too much of it.

10.9

祭于公[1]，不宿肉[2]。祭肉不出三日[3]。出三日不食之矣。

【中译文】

参加国君祭祀典礼分到的肉，不能过夜。平常祭祀用过的肉不能超过三天。超过了三天就不要吃它了。

【注释】

1 祭于公：指士大夫等参加国君举行的祭祀典礼。

2 不宿肉："肉"，指"胙肉"，祭祀所用的肉。胙肉一般由祭祀当天清晨特意宰杀的牲畜肉充任，到第二天祭礼完全结束后再分赐给助祭者。故这种胙肉拿回家已是宰杀后的两三天了，不宜再放过夜。

3 祭肉：指自家祭祀所用的肉。

【英译文】

When, having assisted his prince in a sacrifice, he received a present of meat, he did not keep it overnight. He did not eat the meat of a sacrifice which had been kept more than three days.

10.10

食不语，寝不言。

【中译文】

吃饭时不交谈，睡觉时不卧谈。

【英译文】

He did not talk at meals, nor speak when lying in bed.

10.11

虽疏食菜羹[1]，必祭[2]，必齐如也。

【中译文】

虽然是吃粗米饭蔬菜汤，也一定先要祭一祭，一定要像斋戒时那样恭敬严肃。

【注释】

1 疏食：粗食，吃蔬菜和谷米类。羹（gēng）：浓汤。

2 必：底本作“瓜”，据《鲁论语》改。祭：指吃饭前把席上的各种饭菜分别拿出一点，另摆在食器之间，以祭祀远古发明饮食的祖先，表示不忘本。一说，即指一般的祭祖先或祭鬼神。

【英译文】

Though his food was coarse rice and vegetable soup, he would still offer sacrifice first with a grave and respectful air.

10.12

席不正[1]，不坐。

【中译文】

坐席摆放不正确，不坐。

【注释】

1 席：坐席。古代没有椅子凳子，在地上铺上席子以为坐具。

【英译文】

He must not sit on a mat that is not straight.

10.13

乡人饮酒[1]，杖者出[2]，斯出矣。

【中译文】

在举行乡饮酒礼后，要等老年人先离席，自己才可离席。

【注释】

1 乡人饮酒：指举行乡饮酒礼。乡饮酒礼是周代仪礼的一种，可参看《仪礼·乡饮酒礼》及《礼记·乡饮酒义》。

2 杖者：拄拐杖的人，即老年人。我国古代素有尊老敬老的传统美德。周礼讲：“五十杖于家，六十杖于乡，七十杖于国，八十杖于朝。九十者，天子欲有问焉，则就于其家。”对九十岁的老人，连天子有事要问，也要到老人的家里去。

【英译文】

When the men of his village are drinking wine he leaves the feast directly the village-elders have gone out.

10.14

乡人傩[1]，朝服而立于阼阶[2]。

【中译文】

乡人举行迎神驱鬼仪式时，孔子总是穿着朝服站

立在东面的台阶上。

【注释】

1 傩(nuó)：古代在腊月里举行的迎神赛会、驱疫逐鬼的一种仪式。主持者头戴面具，蒙熊皮，穿黑衣，执戈，扬盾，率百隶及童子，敲着鼓，跳着舞，表演驱疫捉鬼的内容。

2 阼(zuò)：大堂前面靠东面的台阶。这里是主人站立以欢迎客人的地方。

【英译文】

When the villagers hold their Expulsion Rite, he puts on his Court dress and stands on the eastern steps.

10.15

问人于他邦[1]，再拜而送之。

【中译文】

孔子托别人代为问候在其他诸侯国的朋友时，要躬身下拜，拜两次，送走所托的人。

【注释】

1 问：问候，问好，这里指托别人代为致意。

【英译文】

When sending a messenger to enquire after someone in another state, he prostrates himself twice while speeding the messenger on his way.

10.16

康子馈药[1]，拜而受之。曰："丘未达[2]，不敢尝。"

【中译文】

季康子向孔子赠药，孔子拜谢而接受了。并说："我对药性不了解，不敢尝。"

【注释】

1 康子：即季康子。参阅《为政篇第二》第二十章。馈(kuì)：赠送。按当时的礼节，接受别人送的药，要当面尝一尝。

2 达：了解，通达事理。

【英译文】

When Ji Kangzi sent him some medicine he prostrated himself and accepted it; but said, As I am not acquainted with its properties, I cannot venture to taste it.

10.17

厩焚[1]。子退朝，曰："伤人乎？"不问马。

【中译文】

马棚失火焚毁了。孔子从朝廷回来，问："伤人了吗？"却不问马怎么样了。

【注释】

1 厩(jiù)：马棚，马房。后也泛指牲口房。

【英译文】

When the stables were burnt down, on returning from Court, The Master said, Was anyone hurt? He did not ask about the horses.

10.18

君赐食，必正席先尝之。君赐腥[1]，必熟而荐之[2]。君赐生，必畜之。侍食于君，君祭，先饭。

【中译文】

国君赐给食物，孔子一定摆正坐席，先尝一尝。国君赐给生肉，一定煮熟了先供奉祖先。国君赐给活的牲畜，一定把它饲养起来。陪同国君一起吃饭，当国君饭前行祭礼时，自己先尝一尝。

【注释】

1 腥：生肉。

2 荐：供奉，进献。这里指煮熟了肉先放在祖先灵位前上供，表示进奉。本章所述各种作法，都是表示敬意。

【英译文】

When his prince sends him a present of food, he must straighten his mat and be the first to taste what has been sent. When what his prince sends is a present of uncooked meat, he must cook it and make a sacrificial offering. When his prince sends a live animal, he must rear it. When he is waiting upon his prince at meal-times, while his prince is making the sacrificial offering, he (the gentleman) tastes the dishes.

10.19

疾，君视之[1]，东首[2]，加朝服，拖绅[3]。

【中译文】

孔子病了，国君来看望，他躺在床上头朝东，把朝服加盖在身上，拖着大束带。

【注释】

1 视：探视，看望。

2 东首：指头朝东。

3 绅(shēn)：朝服的束在腰间的大宽带子。孔子因病卧床，不能穿朝服束腰，故把朝服加盖在身上，把“绅”放在朝服上，拖下带子去，表示对国君的尊敬与迎接。

【英译文】

When he is ill and his prince comes to see him, he has himself laid with his head to the East with his Court robes thrown over him and his sash drawn across the bed.

10.20

君命召，不俟驾行矣[1]。

【中译文】

国君命令召见，孔子不等马车驾好，就先走了。

【注释】

1 俟(sì)：等待。驾：套上马拉车。

【英译文】

When the prince commands his presence he goes straight to the palace without waiting for his carriage to be yoked.

10.21

入太庙，每事问[1]。

【中译文】

孔子走进太庙，对每件事都向主事人仔细询问。

【注释】

1 此章与《八佾篇第三》第十五章文字相似，可参阅。

【英译文】

When the Master entered the Grand, Temple, he asks about every detail.

10.22

朋友死，无所归[1]，曰："于我殡。"

【中译文】

朋友死后，没有人来料理后事。孔子说："由我来负责安葬。"

【注释】

1 归：归宿。这里指后事的安排，如装殓，发丧，埋葬等。

【英译文】

If a friend dies and there are no relatives to fall back on, the Master says, 'The funeral is my affair.'

10.23

朋友之馈，虽车马，非祭肉[1]，不拜。

【中译文】

接受朋友赠送的礼物，即使是车马那样贵重的东西，如果不是祭肉，孔子也不躬身下拜。

【注释】

1 祭肉：指祭祀祖先用的胙肉。为了表示对朋友的祖先像对自己的祖先那样尊敬，在接受祭肉时要拜。

【英译文】

On receiving a present from a friend, even a carriage and horses, he does not prostrate himself. He does so only in the case of sacrificial meat being sent.

10.24

寝不尸[1]，居不容[2]。

【中译文】

睡觉时孔子不是那么僵硬挺直，平日在家坐着，也不像有客人一样面色庄重。

【注释】

1 尸：死尸。这里指像死尸一样展开手足仰卧。

2 居：坐。客：宾客。这里用作动词，指像做客或接待客人那样郑重地坐着——两膝平跪，挺直腰板。这是一种比较费力的姿势。这一句，有的版本是“居不容”。意思则成为：平日居家可以随便一点，不必像祭祀或接待宾客时那样拘谨，使自己的容貌仪态十分郑重严肃。

【英译文】

When sleeping, the Master didn't lie in the posture of a corpse. When at home he did not use ritual attitudes.

10.25

见齐衰者[1]，虽狎[2]，必变。见冕者与瞽者[3]，虽亵[4]，必以貌。凶服者[5]，式之[6]。式负版者[7]。有盛馔[8]，必变色而作[9]。迅雷风烈必变。

【中译文】

孔子见到穿孝服的人，即使关系亲密，态度也变得严肃起来。见到穿官服的和盲人，即使是平日常在一起的熟人或卑贱的人，也一定要在表情上反映出来。乘车时途中遇上穿丧服或送死人衣物的人，便俯下身去伏在车前的横木上。遇上背着国家重要文件的人，也要伏在车前的横木上。做客时遇有丰盛的筵席，一定把态度变得庄重，并且站起身来。遇上迅急的雷电和猛烈的大风，一定要显得沉着冷静。

【注释】

1 齐衰（zī cuī）：孝服。参见《子罕篇第九》第十章。

2 狎（xiá）：亲近，亲密。

3 冕者：穿礼服、官服的人。瞽者：盲人。

4 亵（xiè）：亲近。这里指平日里常见面的、熟悉的人，或卑贱的人。

5 凶服：丧服，也指死人的衣物。

6 式：同“轼”，车前做扶手用的横木。这里指身子向前微俯，伏在横木上，表示同情或尊敬。这是当时社会上的一种礼节。

7 负：背负。版：指国家的图籍（疆域地图，田亩、户口名册等）。

8 盛馔：指盛大丰足的筵席。“馔（zhuàn）”，饮食。

9 作：起立，站起身来。

【英译文】

When appearing before anyone in mourning, however well he knows him, he must put on an altered expression, and when appearing before anyone in sacrificial garb, or a blind man, even informally, he must be sure to adopt the appropriate attitude. On meeting anyone in deep mourning he must bow across the bar of his chariot; he also bows to people carrying planks, When confronted with a particularly choice dainty at a banquet, his countenance should change and he should rise to his feet. Upon hearing a sudden clap of thunder or a violent gust of wind, he must change countenance.

10.26

升车，必正立，执绥[1]。车中，不内顾，不疾言，不亲指[2]。

【中译文】

孔子上车时，总是先站正了身子，拉住扶手带然后登车。在车上，不向车内回头看，不急促地高声说话，不用手指指划划。

【注释】

1 绥（suí）：古代车上设置的拉着上车的绳索。

2 不亲指：不举起自己的手指指划划。这里说的“不内顾，不疾言，不亲指”，都是为了集中精力驾好车，防止自己的容态失礼或使别人产生疑惑。

【英译文】

When getting into a carriage, the Master must stand facing it squarely and holding the mounting-cord. When riding he confines his gaze, does not speak rapidly or point with his fingers.

10.27

色斯举矣[1]。翔而后集。曰：“山梁雌雉[2]，时哉时哉[3]！”子路共之[4]，三嗅而作[5]。

【中译文】

一群野鸡飞起来而孔子神色动了一下。这群野鸡飞翔了一阵之后，停落在树上。孔子说：“山梁上的雌野鸡，过逢其时呀，生逢其时呀！”子路听了这话向野鸡拱了拱手，惊得野鸡长叫了几声，飞走了。

【注释】

1 色斯举矣：“色”，脸色。“举”，鸟飞起来。这句话的文字可能有错漏之处。按后面的文字来推测，可能是说：孔子在山谷中行走，看见一群山鸡在自由飞翔，心有感触，神色动了一下。

2 雉（zhì）：野鸡。

3 时哉：犹言得其时，时运好。孔子见野鸡能自由飞翔下落，自己反没有实现政治抱负的自由，故有此叹。

4 共：同“拱”。拱手，抱拳致敬、致意。

5 三嗅：“嗅”，唐代石经《论语》作“戛(jiá)”。“戛”，是鸟的长叫声。三嗅，指野鸡长叫了几 声。一说，“嗅”，当作“狊(jù)”鸟类张开两翅的样子。作：飞起来。对这一章文字的理解诠释，历来众说纷纭。有 的理解为：几只野鸡看到走过来的人脸色不善(以为要射猎它)，而飞起来了；飞翔了一阵，而后集中落在树上。孔子感慨地说：“山中的雌野鸡能遇险而飞，识时务呀，识时务呀！”子路听了这话，向野鸡拱了拱手表示敬意，野鸡又受了惊，拍打了几下翅膀而飞走了。可参。

【英译文】

(The gentleman) rises and goes at the first sign, and does not 'settle till he has hovered'. (A song) says: The hen-pheasant of the hill-bridge, Knows how to bide its time, to bide its time! When Zi Lu made it an offering, It sniffed three times before it rose.

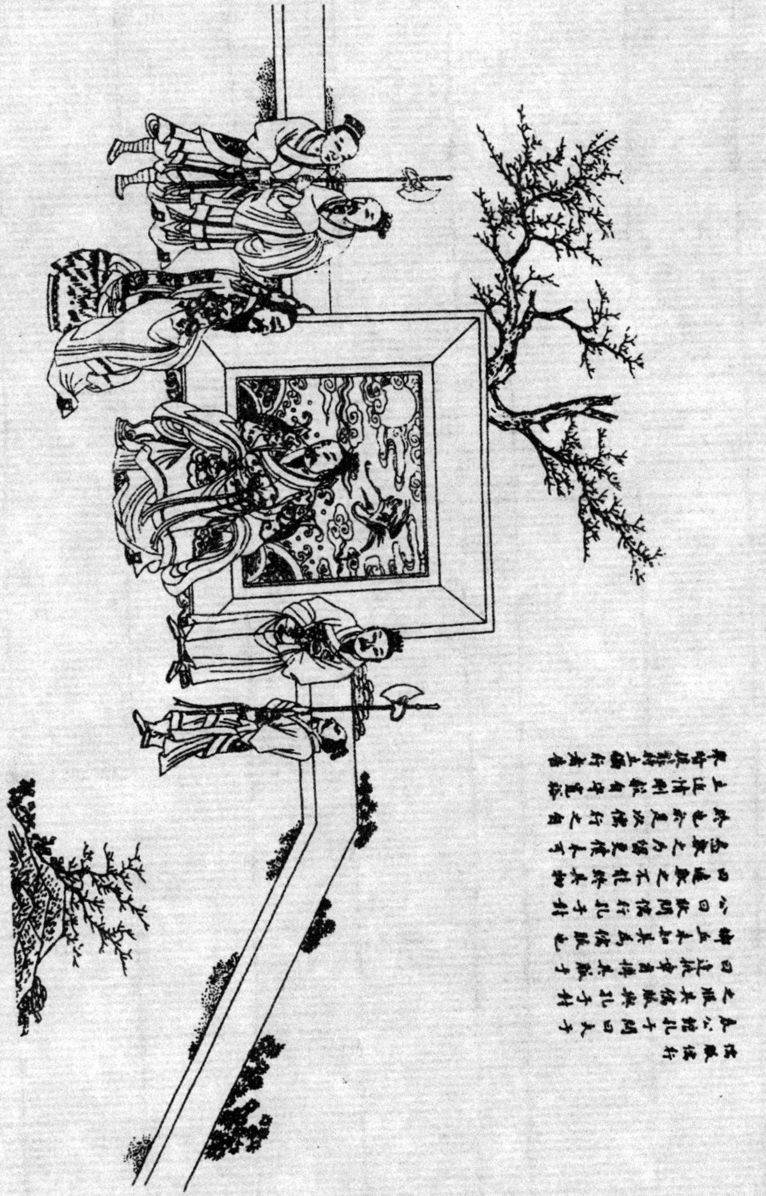

儒服儒行 Confucian Clothes and Behavior

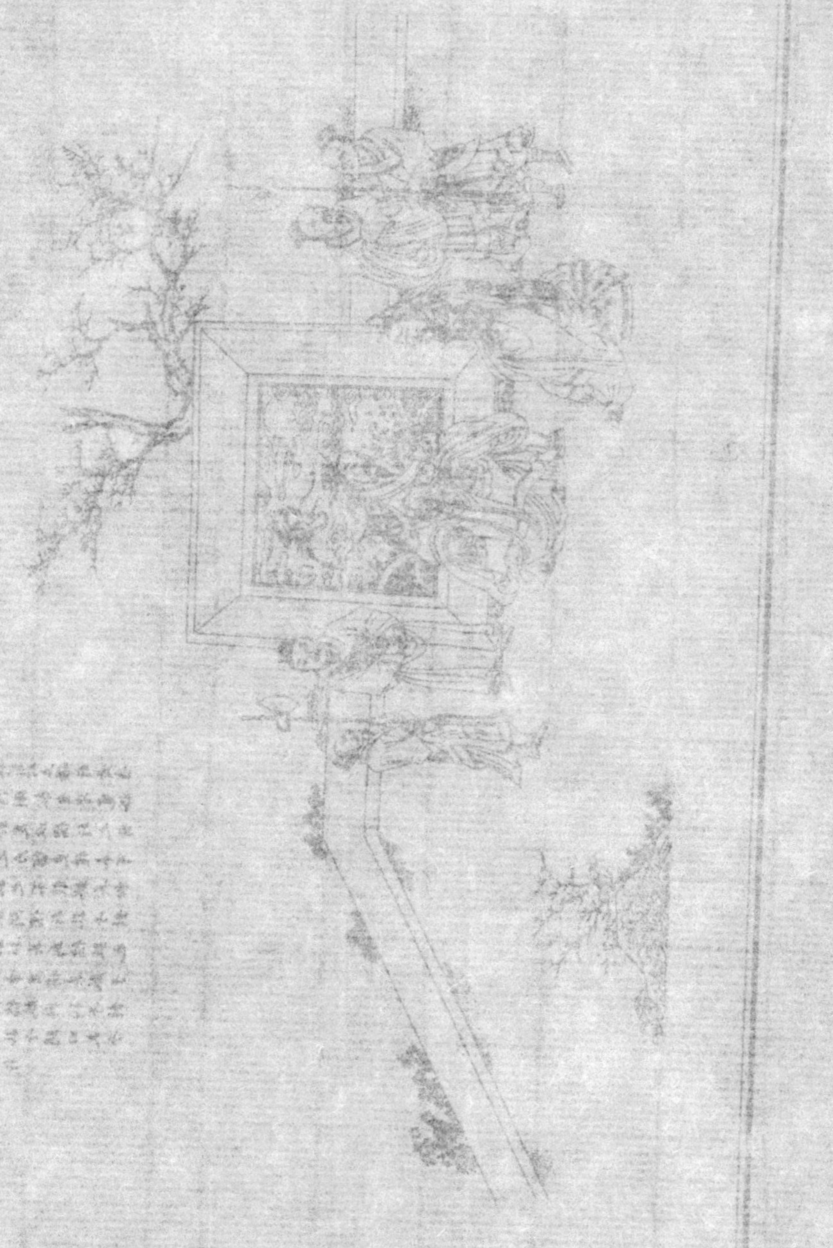